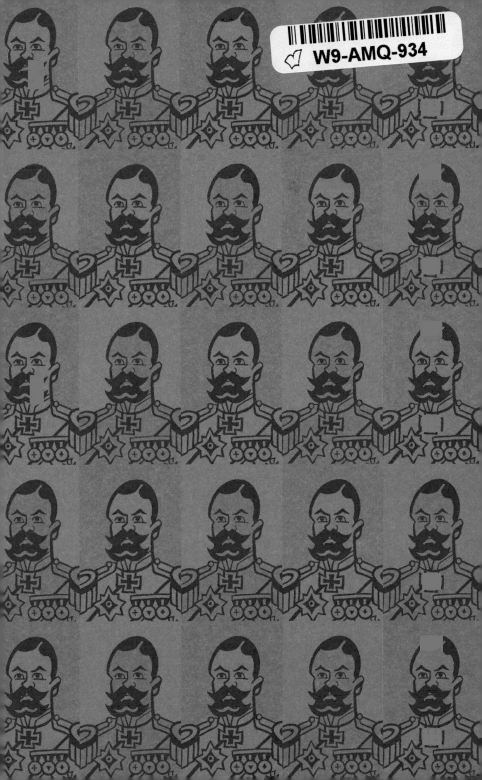

# SUNSHINE SKETCHES

# SUNSHINE SKETCHES OF A LITTLE TOWN

## STEPHEN LEACOCK

DESIGNED & DECORATED BY SETH

SKYHORSE PUBLISHING

CHEF ALPHONSE

ERASMUS ARCHER

PETE ARCHER

J. H. BAGSHA

JOCELYN DRONE

LILIAN DRONE

THEODORA DRONE

GEORGE DUF

PETE GLOVER

WILL HARRISON

MR. HUSSELL

CHRISTIE JOHN

TEDDY MOORE

MR. MORISON

MR. MUDDLESON

HENRY MULLI

PRES. STUDENT

PETER PUPKIN

PUPKIN SR.

MRS. PUPKI

MARJ. TREWLANEY

MRS. THOMPSON

JEFF THORPE

MRS. THORPE

# CONTENTS

# PREFACE

**I** KNOW NO WAY in which a writer may more fittingly introduce his work to the public than by giving a brief account of who and what he is. By this means some of the blame for what he has done is very properly shifted to the extenuating circumstances of his life.

I was born at Swanmoor, Hants, England, on December 30, 1869. I am not aware that there was any particular conjunction of the planets at the time, but should think it extremely likely. My parents migrated to Canada in 1876, and I decided to go with them. My father took up a farm near Lake Simcoe, in Ontario. This was during the hard times of Canadian farming, and my father was just able by great diligence to pay the hired men and, in years of plenty, to raise enough grain to have seed for the next year's crop without buying any. By this process my brothers and I were inevitably driven off the land, and have become professors, business men, and engineers, instead of being able to grow up as farm labourers. Yet I saw enough of farming to speak exuberantly in political addresses of the joy of early rising and the deep sleep, both of body and intellect, that is induced by honest manual toil.

I was educated at Upper Canada College, Toronto, of which I was head boy in 1887. From there I went to the University of Toronto, where I graduated in 1891. At the University I spent my entire time in the acquisition of languages, living, dead, and half-dead, and knew nothing of the outside world. In this diligent pursuit of words I spent about sixteen hours of each day. Very soon after graduation I had forgotten the languages, and found myself intellectually bankrupt. In other words I was what is called a distinguished graduate, and, as such, I took to school teaching as the only trade I could find that need neither experience nor intellect. I spent my time from 1891 to 1899 on the staff of Upper Canada College, an experience which has left me with a profound sympathy for the many gifted and brilliant men who are compelled to spend their lives in the most dreary, the most thankless, and the worst paid profession in the world. I have noted that of my pupils, those who seemed the laziest and the least enamoured of books are now rising to eminence at the bar, in business, and in public life; the really promising boys who took all the prizes are now able with difficulty to earn the wages of a clerk in a summer hotel or a deck hand on a canal boat.

In 1899 I gave up school teaching in disgust, borrowing enough money to live upon for a few months, and went to the University of Chicago to study economics and political science. I was soon appointed to a Fellowship in political economy, and by means of this and some temporary employment by McGill University, I survived until

I took the degree of Doctor of Philosophy in 1903. The meaning of this degree is that the recipient of instruction is examined for the last time in his life, and is pronounced completely full. After this, no new ideas can be imparted to him.

From this time, and since my marriage, which had occurred at this period, I have belonged to the staff of McGill University, first as lecturer in Political Science, and later as head of the department of Economics and Political Science. As this position is one of the prizes of my profession, I am able to regard myself as singularly fortunate. The emolument is so high as to place me distinctly above the policemen, postmen, street-car conductors, and other salaried officials of the neighbourhood, while I am able to mix with the poorer of the business men of the city on terms of something like equality. In point of leisure, I enjoy more in the four corners of a single year than a business man knows in his whole life. I thus have what the business man can never enjoy, an ability to think, and, what is still better, to stop thinking altogether for months at a time.

I have written a number of things in connection with my college life – a book on Political Science, and many essays, magazine articles, and so on. I belong to the Political Science Association of America, to the Royal Colonial Institute, and to the Church of England. These things, surely, are a proof of respectability. I have had some small connection with politics and public life. A few years ago I went all round the British Empire delivering addresses on Imperial organization. When I state that these lectures were followed almost immediately by the Union of South Africa, the Banana Riots in Trinidad, and the Turco-Italian war,

I think the reader can form some idea of their importance. In Canada I belong to the Conservative party, but as yet I have failed entirely in Canadian politics, never having received a contract to build a bridge, or make a wharf, nor to construct even the smallest section of the Transcontinental Railway. This, however, is a form of national ingratitude to which one becomes accustomed in this Dominion.

Apart from my college work, I have written two books, one called "Literary Lapses" and the other "Nonsense Novels." Each of these is published by John Lane (London and New York), and either of them can be obtained, absurd though it sounds, for the mere sum of three shillings and sixpence. Any reader of this preface, for example, ridiculous though it appears, could walk into a bookstore and buy both of these books for seven shillings. Yet these works are of so humorous a character that for many years it was found impossible to print them. The compositors fell back from their task suffocated with laughter and gasping for air. Nothing but the intervention of the linotype machine – or rather, of the kind of men who operate it – made it possible to print these books. Even now people have to be very careful in circulating them, and the books should never be put into the hands of persons not in robust health.

Many of my friends are under the impression that I write these humorous nothings in idle moments when the wearied brain is unable to perform the serious labours of the economist. My own experience is exactly the other way. The writing of solid, instructive stuff fortified by facts and figures is easy enough. There is no trouble in writing a scientific treatise on the folk-lore of Central China, or a statistical enquiry into the declining population of Prince Edward Island. But to write something out of one's own mind, worth reading for its own sake, is an arduous contrivance only to be achieved in fortunate moments, few and far between. Personally, I would sooner have written "Alice in Wonderland" than the whole Encyclopaedia Britannica.

In regard to the present work I must disclaim at once all intentions of trying to do anything so ridiculously easy as writing about a real place and real people. Mariposa is not a real town. On the contrary, it is about seventy or eighty of them. You may find them all the way from Lake Superior to the sea, with the same square streets and the same maple trees and the same churches and hotels, and everywhere the sunshine of the land of hope.

Similarly, the Reverend Mr. Drone is not one person, but about eight or ten. To make him I clapped the gaiters of one ecclesiastic round the legs of another, added the sermons of a third and the character of a fourth, and so let him start on his way in the book to pick up such individual attributes as he might find for himself. Mullins and Bagshaw and Judge Pepperleigh and the rest are, it is true, personal friends of mine. But I have known them in such a variety of forms, with such alternations of tall and short, dark and fair, that, individually, I should have much ado to know them. Mr. Pupkin is found whenever a Canadian bank opens a branch in a county town and needs a teller. As for Mr. Smith, with his two hundred and eighty pounds, his hoarse voice, his loud check suit, his diamonds, the roughness of his address and the goodness of his heart, – all of this is known by everybody to be a necessary and universal adjunct of the hotel business.

The inspiration of the book, – a land of hope and sunshine where little towns spread their square streets and their trim maple trees beside placid lakes almost within echo of the primeval forest, – is large enough. If it fails in its portrayal of the scenes and the country that it depicts the fault lies rather with an art that is deficient than in an affection that is wanting.

Stephen Leacock.

*McGill University,*
*June, 1912.*

JOS. SMITH,
PROP.

# THE HOSTELRY OF MR. SMITH

I DON'T KNOW whether you know Mariposa. If not, it is of no consequence, for if you know Canada at all, you are probably well acquainted with a dozen towns just like it.

There it lies in the sunlight, sloping up from the little lake that spreads out at the foot of the hillside on which the town is built. There is a wharf beside the lake, and lying alongside of it a steamer that is tied to the wharf with two ropes of about the same size as they use on the Lusitania. The steamer goes nowhere in particular, for the lake is landlocked and there is no navigation for the Mariposa Belle except to "run trips" on the first of July and the Queen's Birthday, and to take excursions of the Knights of Pythias and the Sons of Temperance to and from the Local Option Townships.

In point of geography the lake is called Lake Wissanotti and the river running out of it the Ossawippi, just as the main street of Mariposa is called Missinaba Street and the county Missinaba County. But these names do not really matter. Nobody uses them. People simply speak of the "lake" and the "river" and the "main street," much in the same way as they always call the Continental Hotel, "Pete Robinson's" and the Pharmaceutical Hall, "Eliot's Drug Store." But I suppose this is just the same in every one else's town as in mine, so I need lay no stress on it.

The town, I say, has one broad street that runs up from the lake, commonly called the Main Street. There is no doubt about its width. When Mariposa was laid out there was none of that shortsightedness which is seen in the cramped dimensions of Wall Street and Piccadilly. Missinaba Street is so wide that if you were to roll Jeff Thorpe's barber shop over on its face it wouldn't reach half way across. Up and down the Main Street are telegraph poles of cedar of colossal thickness, standing at a variety of angles and carrying rather more wires than are commonly seen at a transatlantic cable station.

On the Main Street itself are a number of buildings of extraordinary importance, – Smith's Hotel and the Continental and the Mariposa House, and the two banks (the Commercial and the Exchange), to say nothing of McCarthy's Block (erected in 1878), and Glover's Hardware Store with the Oddfellows' Hall above it. Then on the "cross" street that intersects Missinaba Street at the main corner there is the Post Office and the Fire Hall and the Young Men's Christian Association and the office of the Mariposa Newspacket, – in fact, to the eye of discernment a perfect jostle of public institutions comparable only to Threadneedle Street or Lower Broadway. On all the side streets there are maple trees and broad sidewalks,

trim gardens with upright calla lilies, houses with veran-
dahs, which are here and there being replaced by residences
with piazzas.

To the careless eye the scene on the Main Street of a
summer afternoon is one of deep and unbroken peace.
The empty street sleeps in the sunshine. There is a horse
and buggy tied to the hitching post in front of Glover's
hardware store. There is, usually and commonly, the burly
figure of Mr. Smith, proprietor of Smith's Hotel, standing
in his chequered waistcoat on the steps of his hostelry, and
perhaps, further up the street, Lawyer Macartney going
for his afternoon mail, or the Rev. Mr. Drone, the Rural
Dean of the Church of England Church, going home to
get his fishing rod after a mothers' auxiliary meeting.

But this quiet is mere appearance. In reality, and to
those who know it, the place is a perfect hive of activity.
Why, at Netley's butcher shop (established in 1882) there
are no less than four men working on the sausage machines
in the basement; at the Newspacket office there are as
many more job-printing; there is a long distance telephone
with four distracting girls on high stools wearing steel
caps and talking incessantly; in the offices in McCarthy's
Block are dentists and lawyers with their coats off, ready
to work at any moment; and from the big planing factory
down beside the lake where the railroad siding is, you
may hear all through the hours of the summer afternoon
the long-drawn music of the running saw.

Busy – well, I should think so! Ask any of its inhabitants if Mariposa isn't a busy, hustling, thriving town. Ask
Mullins, the manager of the Exchange Bank, who comes
hustling over to his office from the Mariposa House every

day at 10.30 and has scarcely time all morning to go out
and take a drink with the manager of the Commercial; or
ask – well, for the matter of that, ask any of them if they
ever knew a more rushing go-a-head town than Mariposa.

Of course if you come to the place fresh from New
York, you are deceived. Your standard of vision is all
astray. You do think the place is quiet. You do imagine
that Mr. Smith is asleep merely because he closes his eyes
as he stands. But live in Mariposa for six months or a year
and then you will begin to understand it better; the buildings get higher and higher; the Mariposa House grows
more and more luxurious; McCarthy's Block towers to the
sky; the buses roar and hum to the station; the trains
shriek; the traffic multiplies; the people move faster and
faster; a dense crowd swirls to and fro in the post-office
and the five and ten cent store – and amusements! Well,
now! Lacrosse, baseball, excursions, dances, the Fireman's
Ball every winter and the Catholic picnic every summer;
and music – the town band in the park every Wednesday
evening, and the Oddfellows' brass band on the street
every other Friday; the Mariposa Quartette, the Salvation
Army – why, after a few months' residence you begin to
realize that the place is a mere mad round of gaiety.

In point of population, if one must come down to
figures, the Canadian census puts the numbers every time
at something round 5,000. But it is very generally understood in Mariposa that the census is largely the outcome
of malicious jealousy. It is usual that after the census the
editor of the Mariposa Newspacket makes a careful re-
estimate (based on the data of relative non-payment of
subscriptions), and brings the population up to 6,000.

After that the Mariposa Times-Herald makes an estimate that runs the figures up to 6,500. Then Mr. Gingham, the undertaker, who collects the vital statistics for the provincial government, makes an estimate from the number of what he calls the "demised" as compared with the less interesting persons who are still alive, and brings the population to 7,000. After that somebody else works it out that it's 7,500; then the man behind the bar of the Mariposa House offers to bet the whole room that there are 9,000 people in Mariposa. That settles it, and the population is well on the way to 10,000, when down swoops the federal census taker on his next round and the town has to begin all over again.

Still, it is a thriving town and there is no doubt of it. Even the transcontinental railways, as any townsman will tell you, run through Mariposa. It is true that the trains mostly go through at night and don't stop. But in the wakeful silence of the summer night you may hear the long whistle of the through train for the west as it tears through Mariposa, rattling over the switches and past the semaphores and ending in a long, sullen roar as it takes the trestle bridge over the Ossawippi. Or, better still, on a winter evening about eight o'clock you will see the long row of the Pullmans and diners of the night express going north to the mining country, the windows flashing with brilliant light, and within them a vista of cut glass and snow-white table linen, smiling negroes and millionaires with napkins at their chins whirling past in the driving snowstorm.

I can tell you the people of Mariposa are proud of the trains, even if they don't stop! The joy of being on the main line lifts the Mariposa people above the level of their neighbours in such places as Tecumseh and Nichols Corners into the cosmopolitan atmosphere of through traffic and the larger life. Of course, they have their own train, too – the Mariposa Local, made up right there in the station yard, and running south to the city a hundred miles away. That, of course, is a real train, with a box stove on end in the passenger car, fed with cordwood upside down, and with seventeen flat cars of pine lumber set between the passenger car and the locomotive so as to give the train its full impact when shunting.

Outside of Mariposa there are farms that begin well but get thinner and meaner as you go on, and end sooner or later in bush and swamp and the rock of the north country. And beyond that again, as the background of it all, though it's far away, you are somehow aware of the great pine woods of the lumber country reaching endlessly into the north.

Not that the little town is always gay or always bright in the sunshine. There never was such a place for changing its character with the season. Dark enough and dull it seems of a winter night, the wooden sidewalks creaking with the frost, and the lights burning dim behind the shop windows. In olden times the lights were coal oil lamps; now, of course, they are, or are supposed to be, electricity, – brought from the power house on the lower Ossawippi nineteen miles away. But, somehow, though it starts off as electricity from the Ossawippi rapids, by the time it gets to Mariposa and filters into the little bulbs behind the frosty windows of the shops, it has turned into coal oil again, as yellow and bleared as ever.

After the winter, the snow melts and the ice goes out

of the lake, the sun shines high and the shanty-men come down from the lumber woods and lie round drunk on the sidewalk outside of Smith's Hotel – and that's spring time. Mariposa is then a fierce, dangerous lumber town, calculated to terrorize the soul of a newcomer who does not understand that this also is only an appearance and that presently the rough-looking shanty-men will change their clothes and turn back again into farmers.

Then the sun shines warmer and the maple trees come out and Lawyer Macartney puts on his tennis trousers, and that's summer time. The little town changes to a sort of summer resort. There are visitors up from the city. Every one of the seven cottages along the lake is full. The Mariposa Belle churns the waters of the Wissanotti into foam as she sails out from the wharf, in a cloud of flags, the band playing and the daughters and sisters of the Knights of Pythias dancing gaily on the deck.

That changes too. The days shorten. The visitors disappear. The golden rod beside the meadow droops and withers on its stem. The maples blaze in glory and die. The evening closes dark and chill, and in the gloom of the main corner of Mariposa the Salvation Army around a naphtha lamp lift up the confession of their sins – and that is autumn. Thus the year runs its round, moving and changing in Mariposa, much as it does in other places.

If, then, you feel that you know the town well enough to be admitted into the inner life and movement of it, walk down this June afternoon half way down the Main Street – or, if you like, half way up from the wharf – to where Mr. Smith is standing at the door of his hostelry. You will feel as you draw near that it is no ordinary man that you approach. It is not alone the huge bulk of Mr. Smith (two hundred and eighty pounds as tested on Netley's scales). It is not merely his costume, though the chequered waistcoat of dark blue with a flowered pattern forms, with his shepherd's plaid trousers, his grey spats and patent-leather boots, a colour scheme of no mean order. Nor is it merely Mr. Smith's finely mottled face. The face, no doubt, is a notable one, – solemn, inexpressible, unreadable, the face of the heaven-born hotel keeper. It is more than that. It is the strange dominating personality of the man that somehow holds you captive. I know nothing in history to compare with the position of Mr. Smith among those who drink over his bar, except, though in a lesser degree, the relation of the Emperor Napoleon to the Imperial Guard.

When you meet Mr. Smith first you think he looks like an over-dressed pirate. Then you begin to think him a character. You wonder at his enormous bulk. Then the utter hopelessness of knowing what Smith is thinking by merely looking at his features gets on your mind and makes the Mona Lisa seem an open book and the ordinary human countenance as superficial as a puddle in the sunlight. After you have had a drink in Mr. Smith's bar, and he has called you by your Christian name, you realize that you are dealing with one of the greatest minds in the hotel business.

Take, for instance, the big sign that sticks out into the street above Mr. Smith's head as he stands. What is on it? "JOS. SMITH, PROP." Nothing more, and yet the thing was a flash of genius. Other men who had had the hotel before Mr. Smith had called it by such feeble names as the Royal Hotel and the Queen's and the Alexandria. Every one of them failed. When Mr. Smith took over the hotel he simply put up the sign with "JOS. SMITH, PROP.," and then stood underneath in the sunshine as a living proof that a man who weighs nearly three hundred pounds is the natural king of the hotel business.

But on this particular afternoon, in spite of the sunshine and deep peace, there was something as near to profound concern and anxiety as the features of Mr. Smith were ever known to express.

The moment was indeed an anxious one. Mr. Smith was awaiting a telegram from his legal adviser who had that day journeyed to the county town to represent the proprietor's interest before the assembled License Commissioners. If you know anything of the hotel business at all, you will understand that as beside the decisions of the License Commissioners of Missinaba County, the opinion of the Lords of the Privy Council are mere trifles.

The matter in question was very grave. The Mariposa Court had just fined Mr. Smith for the second time for selling liquors after hours. The Commissioners, therefore, were entitled to cancel the license.

Mr. Smith knew his fault and acknowledged it. He had broken the law. How he had come to do so, it passed his imagination to recall. Crime always seems impossible in retrospect. By what sheer madness of the moment could he have shut up the bar on the night in question, and shut Judge Pepperleigh, the district judge in Missinaba County, outside of it? The more so inasmuch as the closing up of the bar under the rigid license law of the province was a matter that the proprietor never trusted to any hands but his own. Punctually every night at 11 o'clock Mr. Smith strolled from the desk of the "rotunda" to the door of the bar. If it seemed properly full of people and all was bright and cheerful, then he closed it. If not, he kept it open a few minutes longer till he had enough people inside to warrant closing. But never, never unless he was assured that Pepperleigh, the judge of the court, and Macartney, the prosecuting attorney, were both safely in the bar, or the bar parlour, did the proprietor venture to close up. Yet on this fatal night Pepperleigh and Macartney had been shut out – actually left on the street without a drink, and compelled to hammer and beat at the street door of the bar to gain admittance.

This was the kind of thing not to be tolerated. Either a hotel must be run decently or quit. An information was laid next day and Mr. Smith convicted in four minutes, his lawyers practically refusing to plead. The Mariposa court, when the presiding judge was cold sober, and it had the force of public opinion behind it, was a terrible engine of retributive justice.

So no wonder that Mr. Smith awaited with anxiety the message of his legal adviser.

He looked alternately up the street and down it again, hauled out his watch from the depths of his embroidered pocket, and examined the hour hand and the minute hand and the second hand with frowning scrutiny.

Then wearily, and as one mindful that a hotel man is ever the servant of the public, he turned back into the hotel.

"Billy," he said to the desk clerk, "if a wire comes bring it into the bar parlour."

The voice of Mr. Smith is of a deep guttural such as Plancon or Edouard de Reske might have obtained had they had the advantages of the hotel business. And with that, Mr. Smith, as was his custom in off moments, joined his guests in the back room. His appearance, to the untrained eye, was merely that of an extremely stout hotel-keeper walking from the rotunda to the back bar. In reality, Mr. Smith was on the eve of one of the most brilliant and daring strokes ever effected in the history of licensed liquor. When I say that it was out of the agitation of this situation that Smith's Ladies' and Gent's Café originated, anybody who knows Mariposa will understand the magnitude of the moment.

Mr. Smith, then, moved slowly from the doorway of the hotel through the "rotunda," or more simply the front room with the desk and the cigar case in it, and so to the bar and thence to the little room or back bar behind it. In this room, as I have said, the brightest minds of Mariposa might commonly be found in the quieter part of a summer afternoon.

To-day there was a group of four who looked up as Mr. Smith entered, somewhat sympathetically, and evidently aware of the perplexities of the moment.

Henry Mullins and George Duff, the two bank managers, were both present. Mullins is a rather short, rather round, smooth-shaven man of less than forty, wearing one of those round banking suits of pepper and salt, with a round banking hat of hard straw, and with the kind of gold tie-pin and heavy watch-chain and seals necessary to inspire confidence in matters of foreign exchange. Duff is just as round and just as short, and equally smoothly shaven, while his seals and straw hat are calculated to prove that the Commercial is just as sound a bank as the Exchange. From the technical point of view of the banking

JUDGE
PEPPERLEIGH

business, neither of them had any objection to being in Smith's Hotel or to taking a drink as long as the other was present. This, of course, was one of the cardinal principles of Mariposa banking.

Then there was Mr. Diston, the high school teacher, commonly known as the "one who drank." None of the other teachers ever entered a hotel unless accompanied by a lady or protected by a child. But as Mr. Diston was known to drink beer on occasions and to go in and out of the Mariposa House and Smith's Hotel, he was looked upon as a man whose life was a mere wreck. Whenever the School Board raised the salaries of the other teachers, fifty or sixty dollars per annum at one lift, it was well understood that public morality wouldn't permit of an increase for Mr. Diston.

Still more noticeable, perhaps, was the quiet, sallow looking man dressed in black, with black gloves and with black silk hat heavily craped and placed hollow-side-up on a chair. This was Mr. Golgotha Gingham, the undertaker of Mariposa, and his dress was due to the fact that he had just come from what he called an "interment." Mr. Gingham had the true spirit of his profession, and such words as "funeral" or "coffin" or "hearse" never passed his lips. He spoke always of "interments," of "caskets," and "coaches," using terms that were calculated rather to bring out the majesty and sublimity of death than to parade its horrors.

To be present at the hotel was in accord with Mr. Gingham's general conception of his business. No man had ever grasped the true principles of undertaking more thoroughly than Mr. Gingham. I have often heard him explain that to associate with the living, uninteresting though they appear, is the only way to secure the custom of the dead.

"Get to know people really well while they are alive," said Mr. Gingham; "be friends with them, close friends, and then when they die you don't need to worry. You'll get the order every time."

So, naturally, as the moment was one of sympathy, it was Mr. Gingham who spoke first.

"What'll you do, Josh," he said, "if the Commissioners go against you?"

"Boys," said Mr. Smith, "I don't rightly know. If I have to quit, the next move is to the city. But I don't reckon that I will have to quit. I've got an idee that I think's good every time."

"Could you run a hotel in the city?" asked Mullins.

"I could," said Mr. Smith. "I'll tell you. There's big things doin' in the hotel business right now, big chances if you go into it right. Hotels in the city is branching out. Why, you take the dining-room side of it," continued Mr. Smith, looking round at the group, "there's thousands in it. The old plan's all gone. Folks won't eat now in an ordinary dining-room with a high ceiling and windows. You have to get 'em down underground in a room with no windows and lots of sawdust round and waiters that can't speak English. I seen them places last time I was in the city. They call 'em Rats' Coolers. And for light meals they want a Caff, a real French Caff, and for folks that come in late another place that they call a Girl Room that don't shut up at all. If I go to the city that's the kind of place I mean to run. What's yours, Gol? It's on the house."

And it was just at the moment when Mr. Smith said this that Billy, the desk-clerk, entered the room with the telegram in his hand.

But stop – it is impossible for you to understand the anxiety with which Mr. Smith and his associates awaited the news from the Commissioners, without first realizing the astounding progress of Mr. Smith in the three past years, and the pinnacle of public eminence to which he had attained.

Mr. Smith had come down from the lumber country of the Spanish River, where the divide is toward the Hudson Bay, – "back north" as they called it in Mariposa.

He had been, it was said, a cook in the lumber shanties. To this day Mr. Smith can fry an egg on both sides with a lightness of touch that is the despair of his own "help."

After that, he had run a river driver's boarding-house.

After that, he had taken a food contract for a gang of railroad navvies on the transcontinental.

After that, of course, the whole world was open to him.

He came down to Mariposa and bought out the "inside" of what had been the Royal Hotel.

Those who are educated understand that by the "inside" of a hotel is meant everything except the four outer walls of it – the fittings, the furniture, the bar, Billy the desk clerk, the three dining-room girls, and above all the license granted by King Edward VII, and ratified further by King George, for the sale of intoxicating liquors.

Till then the Royal had been a mere nothing. As "Smith's Hotel" it broke into a blaze of effulgence.

From the first, Mr. Smith, as a proprietor, was a wild, rapturous success.

He had all the qualifications.

He weighed two hundred and eighty pounds.

He could haul two drunken men out of the bar each by the scruff of the neck without the faintest anger or excitement.

He carried money enough in his trousers pockets to start a bank, and spent it on anything, bet it on anything, and gave it away in handfuls.

He was never drunk, and, as a point of chivalry to his customers, never quite sober. Anybody was free of the hotel who cared to come in. Anybody who didn't like it could go out. Drinks of all kinds cost five cents, or six for a quarter. Meals and beds were practically free. Any persons foolish enough to go to the desk and pay for them, Mr. Smith charged according to the expression of their faces.

At first the loafers and the shanty men settled down on the place in a shower. But that was not the "trade" that Mr. Smith wanted. He knew how to get rid of them. An army of charwomen, turned into the hotel, scrubbed it from top to bottom. A vacuum cleaner, the first seen in Mariposa, hissed and screamed in the corridors. Forty brass beds were imported from the city, not, of course, for the guests to sleep in, but to keep them out. A bar-tender with a starched coat and wicker sleeves was put behind the bar.

The loafers were put out of business. The place had become too "high toned" for them.

To get the high class trade, Mr. Smith set himself to dress the part. He wore wide cut coats of filmy serge, light as gossamer; chequered waistcoats with a pattern for every day in the week; fedora hats light as autumn leaves; four-in-hand ties of saffron and myrtle green with a diamond pin the size of a hazelnut. On his fingers there were as many gems as would grace a native prince of India; across his waistcoat lay a gold watch-chain in huge square links and in his pocket a gold watch that weighed a pound and a half and marked minutes, seconds, and quarter seconds. Just to look at Josh Smith's watch brought at least ten men to the bar every evening.

Every morning Mr. Smith was shaved by Jefferson Thorpe, across the way. All that art could do, all that Florida water could effect, was lavished on his person.

Mr. Smith became a local character. Mariposa was at his feet. All the reputable businessmen drank at Mr. Smith's bar, and in the little parlour behind it you might find at any time a group of the brightest intellects in the town.

Not but what there was opposition at first. The clergy, for example, who accepted the Mariposa House and the Continental as a necessary and useful evil, looked askance at the blazing lights and the surging crowd of Mr. Smith's saloon. They preached against him. When the Rev. Dean Drone led off with a sermon on the text "Lord be merciful even unto this publican Matthew Six," it was generally understood as an invitation to strike Mr. Smith dead. In the same way the sermon at the Presbyterian church the week after was on the text "Lo what now doeth Abiram in the land of Melchisideck Kings Eight and Nine?" and it was perfectly plain that what was meant was, "Lo, what is Josh Smith doing in Mariposa?"

But this opposition had been countered by a wide and sagacious philanthropy. I think Mr. Smith first got the idea of that on the night when the steam merry-go-round came to Mariposa. Just below the hostelry, on an empty lot, it whirled and whistled, steaming forth its tunes on the summer evening while the children crowded round it in hundreds. Down the street strolled Mr. Smith, wearing a soft fedora to indicate that it was evening.

"What d'you charge for a ride, boss?" said Mr. Smith.

"Two for a nickel," said the man.

"Take that," said Mr. Smith, handing out a ten-dollar bill from a roll of money, "and ride the little folks free all evening."

That night the merry-go-round whirled madly till after midnight, freighted to capacity with Mariposa children, while up in Smith's Hotel, parents, friends and admirers, as the news spread, were standing four deep along the bar. They sold forty dollars' worth of lager alone that night, and Mr. Smith learned, if he had not already suspected it, the blessedness of giving.

The uses of philanthropy went further. Mr. Smith subscribed to everything, joined everything, gave to everything. He became an Oddfellow, a Forester, A Knight of Pythias and a Workman. He gave a hundred dollars to the Mariposa Hospital and a hundred dollars to the Young Men's Christian Association.

He subscribed to the Ball Club, the Lacrosse Club, the Curling Club, to anything, in fact, and especially to all those things which needed premises to meet in and grew thirsty in their discussions.

As a consequence the Oddfellows held their annual banquet at Smith's Hotel and the Oyster Supper of the Knights of Pythias was celebrated in Mr. Smith's dining-room.

Even more effective, perhaps, were Mr. Smith's secret benefactions, the kind of giving done by stealth of which not a soul in town knew anything, often, for a week after it was done. It was in this way that Mr. Smith put the new font in Dean Drone's church, and handed over a hundred dollars to Judge Pepperleigh for the unrestrained use of the Conservative party.

So it came about that, little by little, the antagonism had died down. Smith's Hotel became an accepted institution in Mariposa. Even the temperance people were proud of Mr. Smith as a sort of character who added distinction to the town. There were moments, in the earlier quiet of the morning, when Dean Drone would go so far as to step in to the "rotunda" and collect a subscription. As for the Salvation Army, they ran in and out all the time unreproved.

On only one point difficulty still remained. That was the closing of the bar. Mr. Smith could never bring his mind to it, – not as a matter of profit, but as a point of honour. It was too much for him to feel that Judge Pepperleigh might be out on the sidewalk thirsty at midnight, that the night hands of the Times-Herald on Wednesday might be compelled to go home dry. On this point Mr. Smith's moral code was simplicity itself, – do what is right and take the consequences. So the bar stayed open.

Every town, I suppose, has its meaner spirits. In every genial bosom some snake is warmed, – or, as Mr. Smith put it to Golgotha Gingham – "there are some fellers even in this town skunks enough to inform."

At first the Mariposa court quashed all indictments. The presiding judge, with his spectacles on and a pile of books in front of him, threatened the informer with the penitentiary. The whole bar of Mariposa was with Mr. Smith. But by sheer iteration the informations had proved successful. Judge Pepperleigh learned that Mr. Smith had subscribed a hundred dollars for the Liberal party and at once fined him for keeping open after hours. That made one conviction. On the top of this had come the untoward incident just mentioned and that made two. Beyond that was the deluge. This then was the exact situation when Billy, the desk clerk, entered the back bar with the telegram in his hand.

"Here's your wire, sir," he said.

"What does it say?" said Mr. Smith.

He always dealt with written documents with a fine air of detachment. I don't suppose there were ten people in Mariposa who knew that Mr. Smith couldn't read.

Billy opened the message and read, "Commissioners give you three months to close down."

"Let me read it," said Mr. Smith, "that's right, three months to close down."

There was dead silence when the message was read. Everybody waited for Mr. Smith to speak. Mr. Gingham instinctively assumed the professional air of hopeless melancholy.

As it was afterwards recorded, Mr. Smith stood and "studied" with the tray in his hand for at least four minutes. Then he spoke.

"Boys," he said, "I'll be darned if I close down till I'm ready to close down. I've got an idee. You wait and I'll show you."

And beyond that, not another word did Mr. Smith say on the subject.

But within forty-eight hours the whole town knew that something was doing. The hotel swarmed with carpenters, bricklayers and painters. There was an architect up from the city with a bundle of blueprints in his hand. There was an engineer taking the street level with a theodolite, and a gang of navvies with shovels digging like fury as if to dig out the back foundations of the hotel.

"That'll fool 'em," said Mr. Smith.

Half the town was gathered round the hotel crazy with excitement. But not a word would the proprietor say.

Great dray loads of square timber, and two-by-eight pine joists kept arriving from the planing mill. There was a pile of matched spruce sixteen feet high lying by the sidewalk.

Then the excavation deepened and the dirt flew, and the beams went up and the joists across, and all the day from dawn till dusk the hammers of the carpenters clattered away, working overtime at time and a half.

"It don't matter what it costs," said Mr. Smith; "get it done."

Rapidly the structure took form. It extended down the side street, joining the hotel at a right angle. Spacious and graceful it looked as it reared its uprights into the air.

Already you could see the place where the row of windows was to come, a veritable palace of glass, it must be, so wide and commodious were they. Below it, you could see the basement shaping itself, with a low ceiling like a vault and big beams running across, dressed, smoothed, and ready for staining. Already in the street there were seven crates of red and white awning.

And even then nobody knew what it was, and it was not till the seventeenth day that Mr. Smith, in the privacy of the back bar, broke the silence and explained.

"I tell you, boys," he says, "it's a caff – like what they have in the city – a ladies' and gent's caff, and that underneath (what's yours, Mr. Mullins?) is a Rats' Cooler. And when I get her started, I'll hire a French Chief to do the cooking, and for the winter I will put in a 'girl room,' like what they have in the city hotels. And I'd like to see who's going to close her up then."

Within two more weeks the plan was in operation. Not only was the caff built but the very hotel was transformed. Awnings had broken out in a red and white cloud upon its face, its every window carried a box of hanging plants, and above in glory floated the Union Jack. The very stationery was changed. The place was now Smith's Summer Pavilion. It was advertised in the city as Smith's Tourists' Emporium, and Smith's Northern Health Resort. Mr. Smith got the editor of the Times-Herald to write up a circular all about ozone and the Mariposa pine woods, with illustrations of the maskinonge (piscis mariposis) of Lake Wissanotti.

The Saturday after that circular hit the city in July, there were men with fishing rods and landing nets pouring in on every train, almost too fast to register. And if, in the face of that, a few little drops of whiskey were sold over the bar, who thought of it?

But the caff! that, of course, was the crowning glory of the thing, that and the Rats' Cooler below.

Light and cool, with swinging windows open to the air, tables with marble tops, palms, waiters in white coats – it was the standing marvel of Mariposa. Not a soul in the town except Mr. Smith, who knew it by instinct, ever guessed that waiters and palms and marble tables can be rented over the long distance telephone.

Mr. Smith was as good as his word. He got a French Chief with an aristocratic saturnine countenance, and a moustache and imperial that recalled the late Napoleon III. No one knew where Mr. Smith got him. Some people in the town said he was a French marquis. Others said he was a count and explained the difference.

No one in Mariposa had ever seen anything like the caff. All down the side of it were the grill fires, with great pewter dish covers that went up and down on a chain, and you could walk along the row and actually pick out your own cutlet and then see the French marquis throw it on to the broiling iron; you could watch a buckwheat pancake whirled into existence under your eyes and see fowls' legs devilled, peppered, grilled, and tormented till they lost all semblance of the original Mariposa chicken.

Mr. Smith, of course, was in his glory.

"What have you got to-day, Alf?" he would say, as he strolled over to the marquis. The name of the Chief was, I believe Alphonse, but "Alf" was near enough for Mr. Smith.

The marquis would extend to the proprietor the menu, "Voilà, m'sieu, la carte du jour."

Mr. Smith, by the way, encouraged the use of the French language in the caff. He viewed it, of course, solely in its relation to the hotel business, and, I think, regarded it as a recent invention.

"It's comin' in all the time in the city," he said, "and y'aint expected to understand it."

Mr. Smith would take the carte between his finger and thumb and stare at it. It was all covered with such devices as Potage à la Mariposa – Filet Mignon à la proprietaire – Côtellete à la Smith, and so on.

But the greatest thing about the caff were the prices. Therein lay, as everybody saw at once, the hopeless simplicity of Mr. Smith.

The prices stood fast at twenty-five cents a meal. You could come in and eat all they had in the caff for a quarter.

"No, sir," Mr. Smith said stoutly, "I ain't going to try to raise no prices on the public. The hotel's always been a quarter and the caff's a quarter."

Full? Full of people?

Well, I should think so! From the time the caff opened at 11 till it closed at 8.30, you could hardly find a table. Tourists, visitors, travellers, and half the people of Mariposa crowded at the little tables; crockery rattling, glasses tinkling on trays, corks popping, the waiters in their white coats flying to and fro, Alphonse whirling the cutlets and pancakes into the air, and in and through it all, Mr. Smith, in a white flannel suit and a broad crimson sash about his waist. Crowded and gay from morning to night, and even noisy in its hilarity.

Noisy, yes; but if you wanted deep quiet and cool, if you wanted to step from the glare of a Canadian August to the deep shadow of an enchanted glade, – walk down below into the Rats' Cooler. There you had it; dark old beams (who could believe they were put there a month ago?), great casks set on end with legends such as

Amontillado Fino done in gilt on a black ground, tall steins filled with German beer soft as moss, and a German waiter noiseless as moving foam. He who entered the Rats' Cooler at three of a summer afternoon was buried there for the day. Mr. Golgotha Gingham spent anything from four to seven hours there of every day. In his mind the place had all the quiet charm of an interment, with none of its sorrows.

But at night, when Mr. Smith and Billy, the desk clerk, opened up the cash register and figured out the combined losses of the caff and the Rats' Cooler, Mr. Smith would say:

"Billy, just wait till I get the license renood, and I'll close up this damn caff so tight they'll never know what hit her. What did that lamb cost? Fifty cents a pound, was it? I figure it, Billy, that every one of them hogs eats about a dollar's worth a grub for every twenty-five cents they pay on it. As for Alf – by gosh, I'm through with him."

But that, of course, was only a confidential matter as between Mr. Smith and Billy.

I don't know at what precise period it was that the idea of a petition to the License Commissioners first got about the town. No one seemed to know just who suggested it. But certain it was that public opinion began to swing strongly towards the support of Mr. Smith. I think it was perhaps on the day after the big fish dinner that Alphonse cooked for the Mariposa Canoe Club (at twenty cents a head) that the feeling began to find open expression. People said it was a shame that a man like Josh Smith should be run out of Mariposa by three license commissioners. Who were the license commissioners, anyway?

Why, look at the license system they had in Sweden; yes, and in Finland and in South America. Or, for the matter of that, look at the French and Italians, who drink all day and all night. Aren't they all right? Aren't they a musical people? Take Napoleon, and Victor Hugo; drunk half the time, and yet look what they did.

I quote these arguments not for their own sake, but merely to indicate the changing temper of public opinion in Mariposa. Men would sit in the caff at lunch perhaps for an hour and a half and talk about the license question in general, and then go down into the Rats' Cooler and talk about it for two hours more.

It was amazing the way the light broke in in the case of particular individuals, often the most unlikely, and quelled their opposition.

Take, for example, the editor of the Newspacket. I suppose there wasn't a greater temperance advocate in town. Yet Alphonse queered him with an Omelette à la License in one meal.

Or take Pepperleigh himself, the judge of the Mariposa court. He was put to the bad with a game pie, – pâté normand aux fines herbes – the real thing, as good as a trip to Paris in itself. After eating it, Pepperleigh had the common sense to realize that it was sheer madness to destroy a hotel that could cook a thing like that.

In the same way, the secretary of the School Board was silenced with a stuffed duck à la Ossawippi.

Three members of the town council were converted with a Dindon farci à la Josh Smith.

And then, finally, Mr. Diston persuaded Dean Drone to come, and as soon as Mr. Smith and Alphonse saw him they landed him with a fried flounder that even the apostles would have appreciated.

After that, every one knew that the license question was practically settled. The petition was all over the town. It was printed in duplicate at the Newspacket and you could see it lying on the counter of every shop in Mariposa. Some of the people signed it twenty or thirty times.

It was the right kind of document too. It began – "Whereas in the bounty of providence the earth putteth forth her luscious fruits and her vineyards for the delight and enjoyment of mankind –" It made you thirsty just to read it. Any man who read that petition over was wild to get to the Rats' Cooler.

When it was all signed up they had nearly three thousand names on it.

Then Nivens, the lawyer, and Mr. Gingham (as a provincial official) took it down to the county town, and by three o'clock that afternoon the news had gone out from the long distance telephone office that Smith's license was renewed for three years.

Rejoicings! Well, I should think so! Everybody was down wanting to shake hands with Mr. Smith. They told him that he had done more to boom Mariposa than any ten men in town. Some of them said he ought to run for the town council, and others wanted to make him the Conservative candidate for the next Dominion election. The caff was a mere babel of voices, and even the Rats' Cooler was almost floated away from its moorings.

And in the middle of it all, Mr. Smith found time to say to Billy, the desk clerk: "Take the cash registers out of the caff and the Rats' Cooler and start counting up the books."

And Billy said: "Will I write the letters for the palms and the tables and the stuff to go back?"

And Mr. Smith said: "Get 'em written right away."

So all evening the laughter and the chatter and the congratulations went on, and it wasn't till long after midnight that Mr. Smith was able to join Billy in the private room behind the "rotunda." Even when he did, there was a quiet and a dignity about his manner that had never been there before. I think it must have been the new halo of the Conservative candidacy that already radiated from his brow. It was, I imagine, at this very moment that Mr. Smith first realised that the hotel business formed the natural and proper threshold of the national legislature.

"Here's the account of the cash registers," said Billy.

"Let me see it," said Mr. Smith. And he studied the figures without a word.

"And here's the letters about the palms, and here's Alphonse up to yesterday –"

And then an amazing thing happened.

"Billy," said Mr. Smith, "tear 'em up. I ain't going to do it. It ain't right and I won't do it. They got me the license for to keep the caff and I'm going to keep the caff. I don't need to close her. The bar's good for anything from forty to a hundred a day now, with the Rats' Cooler going good, and that caff will stay right here."

And stay it did.

There it stands, mind you, to this day. You've only to step round the corner of Smith's Hotel on the side street and read the sign: LADIES' AND GENT'S CAFÉ, just as large and as imposing as ever.

Mr. Smith said that he'd keep the caff, and when he said a thing he meant it!

Of course there were changes, small changes.

I don't say, mind you, that the fillet de beef that you get there now is perhaps quite up to the level of the filet de boeufs aux champignons of the days of glory.

No doubt the lamb chops in Smith's Caff are often very much the same, nowadays, as the lamb chops of the Mariposa House or the Continental.

Of course, things like Omelette aux Truflcs practically died out when Alphonse went. And, naturally, the leaving of Alphonse was inevitable. No one knew just when he went, or why. But one morning he was gone. Mr. Smith said that "Alf had to go back to his folks in the old country."

So, too, when Alf left, the use of the French language, as such, fell off tremendously in the caff. Even now they use it to some extent. You can still get fillet de beef, and saucisson au juice, but Billy the desk clerk has considerable trouble with the spelling.

The Rats' Cooler, of course, closed down, or rather Mr. Smith closed it for repairs, and there is every likelihood that it will hardly open for three years. But the caff is there. They don't use the grills, because there's no need to, with the hotel kitchen so handy.

The "girl room," I may say, was never opened. Mr. Smith promised it, it is true, for the winter, and still talks of it. But somehow there's been a sort of feeling against it. Every one in town admits that every big hotel in the city has a "girl room" and that it must be all right. Still, there's a certain – well, you know how sensitive opinion is in a place like Mariposa.

JEFF THORPE

# THE
# SPECULATIONS OF
# JEFFERSON THORPE

IT WAS NOT UNTIL the mining boom, at the time when everybody went simply crazy over the Cobalt and Porcupine mines of the new silver country near the Hudson Bay, that Jefferson Thorpe reached what you might call public importance in Mariposa.

Of course everybody knew Jeff and his little barber shop that stood just across the street from Smith's Hotel. Everybody knew him and everybody got shaved there. From early morning, when the commercial travellers off the 6.30 express got shaved into the resemblance of human beings, there were always people going in and out of the barber shop.

Mullins, the manager of the Exchange Bank, took his morning shave from Jeff as a form of resuscitation, with enough wet towels laid on his face to stew him and with Jeff moving about in the steam, razor in hand, as grave as an operating surgeon.

Then, as I think I said, Mr. Smith came in every morning and there was a tremendous outpouring of Florida water and rums, essences and revivers and renovators, regardless of expense. What with Jeff's white coat and Mr. Smith's flowered waistcoat and the red geranium in the window and the Florida water and the double extract of hyacinth, the little shop seemed multi-coloured and luxurious enough for the annex of a Sultan's harem.

But what I mean is that, till the mining boom, Jefferson Thorpe never occupied a position of real prominence in Mariposa. You couldn't, for example, have compared him with a man like Golgotha Gingham, who, as undertaker, stood in a direct relation to life and death, or to Trelawney, the postmaster, who drew money from the Federal Government of Canada, and was regarded as virtually a member of the Dominion Cabinet.

Everybody knew Jeff and liked him, but the odd thing was that till he made money nobody took any stock in his ideas at all. It was only after he made the "clean up" that they came to see what a splendid fellow he was. "Level-headed" I think was the term; indeed in the speech of Mariposa, the highest form of endowment was to have the head set on horizontally as with a theodolite.

As I say, it was when Jeff made money that they saw how gifted he was, and when he lost it, – but still, there's no need to go into that. I believe it's something the same in other places too.

The barber shop, you will remember, stands across the street from Smith's Hotel, and stares at it face to face.

It is one of those wooden structures – I don't know whether you know them – with a false front that sticks up above its real height and gives it an air at once rectangular and imposing. It is a form of architecture much used in

Mariposa and understood to be in keeping with the pretentious and artificial character of modern business. There is a red, white and blue post in front of the shop and the shop itself has a large square window out of proportion to its little flat face.

Painted on the panes of the window is the remains of a legend that once spelt BARBER SHOP, executed with the flourishes that prevailed in the golden age of sign painting in Mariposa. Through the window you can see the geraniums in the window shelf and behind them Jeff Thorpe with his little black skull cap on and his spectacles drooped upon his nose as he bends forward in the absorption of shaving.

As you open the door, it sets in violent agitation a coiled spring up above and a bell that almost rings. Inside, there are two shaving chairs of the heavier, or electrocution pattern, with mirrors in front of them and pigeon holes with individual shaving mugs. There must be ever so many of them, fifteen or sixteen. It is the current supposition of each of Jeff's customers that everyone else but himself uses a separate mug. One corner of the shop is partitioned off and bears the sign: HOT AND COLD BATHS, 50 cents. There has been no bath inside the partition for twenty years – only old newspapers and a mop. Still, it lends distinction somehow, just as do the faded cardboard signs that hang against the mirror with the legends: TURKISH SHAMPOO, 75 cents, and ROMAN MASSAGE, $1.00.

They said commonly in Mariposa that Jeff made money out of the barber shop. He may have, and it may have been that that turned his mind to investment. But it's hard to see how he could. A shave cost five cents, and a hair-cut fifteen (or the two, if you liked, for a quarter), and at that it is hard to see how he could make money, even when he had both chairs going and shaved first in one and then in the other.

You see, in Mariposa, shaving isn't the hurried, perfunctory thing that it is in the city. A shave is looked upon as a form of physical pleasure and lasts anywhere from twenty-five minutes to three-quarters of an hour.

In the morning hours, perhaps, there was a semblance of haste about it, but in the long quiet of the afternoon, as Jeff leaned forward towards the customer and talked to him in a soft confidential monotone, like a portrait painter, the razor would go slower and slower, and pause and stop, move and pause again, till the shave died away into the mere drowse of conversation.

At such hours, the Mariposa barber shop would become a very Palace of Slumber, and as you waited your turn in one of the wooden arm-chairs beside the wall, what with the quiet of the hour, and the low drone of Jeff's conversation, the buzzing of the flies against the window pane and the measured tick of the clock above the mirror, your head sank dreaming on your breast, and the Mariposa Newspacket rustled unheeded on the floor. It makes one drowsy just to think of it!

The conversation, of course, was the real charm of the place. You see, Jefferson's forte, or specialty, was information. He could tell you more things within the compass of a half-hour's shave than you get in days of laborious research in an encyclopaedia. Where he got it all, I don't know, but I am inclined to think it came more or less out of the newspapers.

In the city, people never read the newspapers, not

really, only little bits and scraps of them. But in Mariposa it's different. There they read the whole thing from cover to cover, and they build up on it, in the course of years, a range of acquirement that would put a college president to the blush. Anybody who has ever heard Henry Mullins and Peter Glover talk about the future of China will know just what I mean.

And, of course, the peculiarity of Jeff's conversation was that he could suit it to his man every time. He had a kind of divination about it. There was a certain kind of man that Jeff would size up sideways as he stropped the razor, and in whose ear he would whisper: "I see where Saint Louis has took four straight games off Chicago," – and so hold him fascinated to the end.

In the same way he would say to Mr. Smith: "I see where it says that this 'Flying Squirl' run a dead heat for the King's Plate."

To a humble intellect like mine he would explain in full the relations of the Keesar to the German Rich Dog.

But first and foremost, Jeff's specialty in the way of conversation was finance and the money market, the huge fortunes that a man with the right kind of head could make.

I've known Jefferson to pause in his shaving with the razor suspended in the air as long as five minutes while he described, with his eye half closed, exactly the kind of a head a man needed in order to make a "haul" or a "clean up." It was evidently simply a matter of the head, and as far as one could judge, Jeff's own was the very type required.

I don't know just at what time or how Jefferson first began his speculative enterprises. It was probably in him from the start. There is no doubt that the very idea of such things as Traction Stock and Amalgamated Asbestos went to his head: and whenever he spoke of Mr. Carnegie and Mr. Rockefeller, the yearning tone of his voice made it as soft as lathered soap.

I suppose the most rudimentary form of his speculation was the hens. That was years ago. He kept them out at the back of his house, – which itself stood up a grass plot behind and beyond the barber shop, – and in the old days Jeff would say, with a certain note of pride in his voice, that The Woman had sold as many as two dozen eggs in a day to the summer visitors.

But what with reading about Amalgamated Asbestos and Consolidated Copper and all that, the hens began to seem pretty small business, and, in any case, the idea of two dozen eggs at a cent apiece almost makes one blush. I suppose a good many of us have felt just as Jeff did about our poor little earnings. Anyway, I remember Jeff telling me one day that he could take the whole lot of the hens and sell them off and crack the money into Chicago wheat on margin and turn it over in twenty-four hours. He did it too. Only somehow when it was turned over it came upside down on top of the hens.

After that the hen house stood empty and The Woman had to throw away chicken feed every day, at a dead loss of perhaps a shave and a half. But it made no difference to Jeff, for his mind had floated away already on the possibilities of what he called "displacement" mining on the Yukon.

So you can understand that when the mining boom struck Mariposa, Jefferson Thorpe was in it right from the very start. Why, no wonder; it seemed like the finger of Providence. Here was this great silver country spread out to the north of us, where people had thought there was only a wilderness. And right at our very doors! You could see, as I saw, the night express going north every evening; for all one knew Rockefeller or Carnegie or anyone might be on it! Here was the wealth of Calcutta, as the Mariposa Newspacket put it, poured out at our very feet.

So no wonder the town went wild! All day in the street you could hear men talking of veins, and smelters and dips and deposits and faults, – the town hummed with it like a geology class on examination day. And there were men about the hotels with mining outfits and theodolites and dunnage bags, and at Smith's bar they would hand chunks of rock up and down, some of which would run as high as ten drinks to the pound.

The fever just caught the town and ran through it! Within a fortnight they put a partition down Robertson's Coal and Wood Office and opened the Mariposa Mining Exchange, and just about every man on the Main Street started buying scrip. Then presently young Fizzlechip, who had been teller in Mullins's Bank and that everybody had thought a worthless jackass before, came back from the Cobalt country with a fortune, and loafed round in the Mariposa House in English khaki and a horizontal hat, drunk all the time, and everybody holding him up as an example of what it was possible to do if you tried.

They all went in. Jim Eliot mortgaged the inside of the drug store and jammed it into Twin Tamagami. Pete Glover at the hardware store bought Nippewa stock at thirteen cents and sold it to his brother at seventeen and bought it back in less than a week at nineteen. They didn't care! They took a chance. Judge Pepperleigh put the rest

of his wife's money into Temiskaming Common, and
Lawyer Macartney got the fever, too, and put every cent
that his sister possessed into Tulip Preferred.

And even when young Fizzlechip shot himself in the
back room of the Mariposa House, Mr. Gingham buried
him in a casket with silver handles and it was felt that
there was a Monte Carlo touch about the whole thing.

They all went in – or all except Mr. Smith. You see,
Mr. Smith had come down from there, and he knew all
about rocks and mining and canoes and the north country.
He knew what it was to eat flour-baked dampers under the
lee side of a canoe propped among the underbrush, and to
drink the last drop of whiskey within fifty miles. Mr. Smith
had mighty little use for the north. But what he did do, was
to buy up enough early potatoes to send fifteen carload lots
into Cobalt at a profit of five dollars a bag.

Mr. Smith, I say, hung back. But Jeff Thorpe was in
the mining boom right from the start. He bought in on the
Nippewa mine even before the interim prospectus was out.
He took a "block" of 100 shares of Abbitibbi Development
at fourteen cents, and he and Johnson, the livery stable-
keeper next door, formed a syndicate and got a thousand
shares of Metagami Lake at 3¼ cents and then "unloaded"
them on one of the sausage men at Netley's butcher shop
at a clear cent per cent advance.

Jeff would open the little drawer below the mirror in
the barber shop and show you all kinds and sorts of Cobalt
country mining certificates, – blue ones, pink ones, green
ones, with outlandish and fascinating names on them that
ran clear from the Mattawa to the Hudson Bay.

And right from the start he was confident of winning.

"There ain't no difficulty to it," he said, "there's lots of silver up there in that country and if you buy some here and some there you can't fail to come out somewhere. I don't say," he used to continue, with the scissors open and ready to cut, "that some of the greenhorns won't get bit. But if a feller knows the country and keeps his head level, he can't lose."

Jefferson had looked at so many prospectuses and so many pictures of mines and pine trees and smelters, that I think he'd forgotten that he'd never been in the country. Anyway, what's two hundred miles!

To an onlooker it certainly didn't seem so simple. I never knew the meanness, the trickery, of the mining business, the sheer obstinate determination of the bigger capitalists not to make money when they might, till I heard the accounts of Jeff's different mines. Take the case of Corona Jewel. There was a good mine, simply going to ruin for lack of common sense.

"She ain't been developed," Jeff would say. "There's silver enough in her so you could dig it out with a shovel. She's full of it. But they won't get at her and work her."

Then he'd take a look at the pink and blue certificates of the Corona Jewel and slam the drawer on them in disgust.

Worse than that was the Silent Pine, – a clear case of stupid incompetence! Utter lack of engineering skill was all that was keeping the Silent Pine from making a fortune for its holders.

"The only trouble with that mine," said Jeff, "is they won't go deep enough. They followed the vein down to where it kind o' thinned out and then they quit. If they'd just go right into her good, they'd get it again. She's down there all right."

But perhaps the meanest case of all was the Northern Star. That always seemed to me, every time I heard of it, a straight case for the criminal law. The thing was so evidently a conspiracy.

"I bought her," said Jeff, "at thirty-two, and she stayed right there tight, like she was stuck. Then a bunch of these fellers in the city started to drive her down and they got her pushed down to twenty-four, and I held on to her and they shoved her down to twenty-one. This morning they've got her down to sixteen, but I don't mean to let go. No, sir."

In another fortnight they shoved her, the same unscrupulous crowd, down to nine cents, and Jefferson still held on.

"They're working her down," he admitted, "but I'm holding her."

No conflict between vice and virtue was ever grimmer.

"She's at six," said Jeff, "but I've got her. They can't squeeze me."

A few days after that, the same criminal gang had her down further than ever.

"They've got her down to three cents," said Jeff, "but I'm with her. Yes, sir, they think they can shove her clean off the market, but they can't do it. I've boughten in Johnson's shares, and the whole of Netley's, and I'll stay with her till she breaks."

So they shoved and pushed and clawed her down – that unseen nefarious crowd in the city – and Jeff held on to her and they writhed and twisted at his grip, and then –

And then – well, that's just the queer thing about the mining business. Why, sudden as a flash of lightning, it seemed, the news came over the wire to the Mariposa Newspacket, that they had struck a vein of silver in the Northern Star as thick as a sidewalk, and that the stock had jumped to seventeen dollars a share, and even at that you couldn't get it! And Jeff stood there flushed and half-staggered against the mirror of the little shop, with a bunch of mining scrip in his hand that was worth forty thousand dollars!

Excitement! It was all over the town in a minute. They ran off a news extra at the Mariposa Newspacket, and in less than no time there wasn't standing room in the barber shop, and over in Smith's Hotel they had three extra barkeepers working on the lager beer pumps.

They were selling mining shares on the Main Street in Mariposa that afternoon and people were just clutching for them. Then at night there was a big oyster supper in Smith's caff, with speeches, and the Mariposa band outside.

And the queer thing was that the very next afternoon was the funeral of young Fizzlechip, and Dean Drone had to change the whole text of his Sunday sermon at two days' notice for fear of offending public sentiment.

But I think what Jeff liked best of it all was the sort of public recognition that it meant. He'd stand there in the shop, hardly bothering to shave, and explain to the men in the arm-chairs how he held her, and they shoved her, and he clung to her, and what he'd said to himself – a perfect Iliad – while he was clinging to her.

The whole thing was in the city papers a few days after with a photograph of Jeff, taken specially at Ed Moore's studio (upstairs over Netley's). It showed Jeff sitting among palm trees, as all mining men do, with one hand on his knee, and a dog, one of those regular mining dogs, at his feet, and

MARIPOSA KNIGHTS
OF PYTHIAS BAND

a look of piercing intelligence in his face that would easily account for forty thousand dollars.

I say that the recognition meant a lot to Jeff for its own sake. But no doubt the fortune meant quite a bit to him too on account of Myra.

Did I mention Myra, Jeff's daughter? Perhaps not. That's the trouble with the people in Mariposa; they're all so separate and so different – not a bit like the people in the cities – that unless you hear about them separately and one by one you can't for a moment understand what they're like.

Myra had golden hair and a Greek face and would come bursting through the barber shop in a hat at least six inches wider than what they wear in Paris. As you saw her swinging up the street to the Telephone Exchange in a suit that was straight out of the Delineator and brown American boots, there was style written all over her, – the kind of thing that Mariposa recognised and did homage to. And to see her in the Exchange, – she was one of the four girls that I spoke of, – on her high stool with a steel cap on, – jabbing the connecting plugs in and out as if electricity cost nothing – well, all I mean is that you could understand why it was that the commercial travellers would stand round in the Exchange calling up all sorts of impossible villages, and waiting about so pleasant and genial! – it made one realize how naturally good-tempered men are. And then when Myra would go off duty and Miss Cleghorn, who was sallow, would come on, the commercial men would be off again like autumn leaves.

It just shows the difference between people. There was Myra who treated lovers like dogs and would slap them across the face with a banana skin to show her utter independence. And there was Miss Cleghorn, who was sallow, and who bought a forty cent Ancient History to improve herself: and yet if she'd hit any man in Mariposa with a banana skin, he'd have had her arrested for assault.

Mind you, I don't mean that Myra was merely flippant and worthless. Not at all. She was a girl with any amount of talent. You should have heard her recite "The Raven," at the Methodist Social! Simply genius! And when she acted Portia in the Trial Scene of the Merchant of Venice at the High School concert, everybody in Mariposa admitted that you couldn't have told it from the original.

So, of course, as soon as Jeff made the fortune, Myra had her resignation in next morning and everybody knew that she was to go to a dramatic school for three months in the fall and become a leading actress.

But, as I said, the public recognition counted a lot for Jeff. The moment you begin to get that sort of thing it comes in quickly enough. Brains, you know, are recognized right away. That was why, of course, within a week from this Jeff received the first big packet of stuff from the Cuban Land Development Company, with coloured pictures of Cuba, and fields of bananas, and haciendas and insurrectos with machetes and Heaven knows what. They heard of him, somehow, – it wasn't for a modest man like Jefferson to say how. After all, the capitalists of the world are just one and the same crowd. If you're in it, you're in it, that's all! Jeff realized why it is that of course men like Carnegie or Rockefeller and Morgan all know one another. They have to.

For all I know, this Cuban stuff may have been sent from Morgan himself. Some of the people in Mariposa said yes, others said no. There was no certainty.

Anyway, they were fair and straight, this Cuban crowd that wrote to Jeff. They offered him to come right in and be one of themselves. If a man's got the brains, you may as well recognize it straight away. Just as well write him to be a director now as wait and hesitate till he forces his way into it.

Anyhow, they didn't hesitate, these Cuban people that wrote to Jeff from Cuba – or from a post-office box in New York – it's all the same thing, because Cuba being so near to New York the mail is all distributed from there. I suppose in some financial circles they might have been slower, wanted guarantees of some sort, and so on, but these Cubans, you know, have got a sort of Spanish warmth of heart that you don't see in business men in America, and that touches you. No, they asked no guarantee. Just send the money – whether by express order or by bank draft or cheque, they left that entirely to oneself, as a matter between Cuban gentlemen.

And they were quite frank about their enterprise – bananas and tobacco in the plantation district reclaimed from the insurrectos. You could see it all there in the pictures – tobacco plants and the insurrectos – everything. They made no rash promises, just admitted straight out that the enterprise might realise 400 per cent, or might conceivably make less. There was no hint of more.

So within a month, everybody in Mariposa knew that Jeff Thorpe was "in Cuban lands" and would probably clean up half a million by New Year's. You couldn't have failed to know it. All round the little shop there were pictures of banana groves and the harbour of Havana, and Cubans in white suits and scarlet sashes, smoking cigarettes in the sun and too ignorant to know that you can make four hundred per cent by planting a banana tree.

I liked it about Jeff that he didn't stop shaving. He went on just the same. Even when Johnson, the livery stable man, came in with five hundred dollars and asked him to see if the Cuban Board of Directors would let him put it in, Jeff laid it in the drawer and then shaved him for five cents, in the same old way. Of course, he must have felt proud when, a few days later, he got a letter from the Cuban people, from New York, accepting the money straight off without a single question, and without knowing anything more of Johnson except that he was a friend of Jeff's. They wrote most handsomely. Any friends of Jeff's were friends of Cuba. All money they might send would be treated just as Jeff's would be treated.

One reason, perhaps, why Jeff didn't give up shaving was because it allowed him to talk about Cuba. You see, everybody knew in Mariposa that Jeff Thorpe had sold out of Cobalts and had gone into Cuban Renovated Lands – and that spread round him a kind of halo of wealth and mystery and outlandishness – oh, something Spanish. Perhaps you've felt it about people that you know. Anyhow, they asked him about the climate, and yellow fever and what the negroes were like and all that sort of thing.

"This Cubey, it appears is an island," Jeff would explain. Of course, everybody knows how easily islands lend themselves to making money, – "and for fruit, they say it comes up so fast you can't stop it." And then he would pass into details about the Hash-enders and the resurrectos and technical things like that till it was thought a wonder how he could know it. Still, it was realized that a man with

money has got to know these things. Look at Morgan and
Rockefeller and all the men that make a pile. They know
just as much as Jeff did about the countries where they
make it. It stands to reason.

Did I say that Jeff shaved in the same old way? Not
quite. There was something even dreamier about it now,
and a sort of new element in the way Jeff fell out of his
monotone into lapses of thought that I, for one, misunder-
stood. I thought that perhaps getting so much money, –
well, you know the way it acts on people in the larger cities.
It seemed to spoil one's idea of Jeff that copper and asbestos
and banana lands should form the goal of his thought
when, if he knew it, the little shop and the sunlight of
Mariposa was so much better.

In fact, I had perhaps borne him a grudge for what
seemed to me his perpetual interest in the great capitalists.
He always had some item out of the paper about them.

"I see where this here Carnegie has given fifty thousand dollars for one of them observatories," he would say.

And another day he would pause in the course of
shaving, and almost whisper: "Did you ever *see* this
Rockefeller?"

It was only by a sort of accident that I came to know
that there was another side to Jefferson's speculation that
no one in Mariposa ever knew, or will ever know now.

I knew it because I went in to see Jeff in his house
one night. The house, – I think I said it, – stood out behind
the barber shop. You went out of the back door of the
shop, and through a grass plot with petunias beside it, and
the house stood at the end. You could see the light of the
lamp behind the blind, and through the screen door as you

came along. And it was here that Jefferson used to sit in the evenings when the shop got empty.

There was a round table that The Woman used to lay for supper, and after supper there used to be a chequered cloth on it and a lamp with a shade. And beside it Jeff would sit, with his spectacles on and the paper spread out, reading about Carnegie and Rockefeller. Near him, but away from the table, was The Woman doing needlework, and Myra, when she wasn't working in the Telephone Exchange, was there too with her elbows on the table reading Marie Corelli – only now, of course, after the fortune, she was reading the prospectuses of Dramatic Schools.

So this night, – I don't know just what it was in the paper that caused it, – Jeff laid down what he was reading and started to talk about Carnegie.

"This Carnegie, I bet you, would be worth," said Jeff, closing up his eyes in calculation, "as much as perhaps two million dollars, if you was to sell him up. And this Rockefeller and this Morgan, either of them, to sell them up clean, would be worth another couple of million –"

I may say in parentheses that it was a favourite method in Mariposa if you wanted to get at the real worth of a man, to imagine him clean sold up, put up for auction, as it were. It was the only way to test him.

"And now look at 'em," Jeff went on. "They make their money and what do they do with it? They give it away. And who do they give it to? Why, to those as don't want it, every time. They give it to these professors and to this research and that, and do the poor get any of it? Not a cent and never will."

"I tell you, boys," continued Jeff (there were no boys present, but in Mariposa all really important speeches are addressed to an imaginary audience of boys) – "I tell you, if I was to make a million out of this Cubey, I'd give it straight to the poor, yes, sir – divide it up into a hundred lots of a thousand dollars each and give it to the people that hadn't nothing."

So always after that I knew just what those bananas were being grown for.

Indeed, after that, though Jefferson never spoke of his intentions directly, he said a number of things that seemed to bear on them. He asked me, for instance, one day, how many blind people it would take to fill one of these blind homes and how a feller could get ahold of them. And at another time he asked whether if a feller advertised for some of these incurables a feller could get enough of them to make a showing. I know for a fact that he got Nivens, the lawyer, to draw up a document that was to give an acre of banana land in Cuba to every idiot in Missinaba county.

But still, – what's the use of talking of what Jeff meant to do? Nobody knows or cares about it now.

The end of it was bound to come. Even in Mariposa some of the people must have thought so. Else how was it that Henry Mullins made such a fuss about selling a draft for forty thousand on New York? And why was it that Mr. Smith wouldn't pay Billy, the desk clerk, his back wages when he wanted to put it into Cuba?

Oh yes; some of them must have seen it. And yet when it came it seemed so quiet, – ever so quiet, – not a bit like the Northern Star mine and the oyster supper and the Mariposa band. It is strange how quiet these things look, the other way round.

You remember the Cuban Land frauds in New York – and Porforio Gomez shooting the detective, and him and Maximo Morez getting clear away with two hundred thousand? No, of course you don't; why, even in the city papers it only filled an inch or two of type, and anyway the names were hard to remember. That was Jeff's money – part of it. Mullins got the telegram, from a broker or someone, and he showed it to Jeff just as he was going up the street with an estate agent to look at a big empty lot on the hill behind the town – the very place for these incurables.

And Jeff went back to the shop so quiet – have you ever seen an animal that is stricken through, how quiet it seems to move?

Well, that's how he walked.

And since that, though it's quite a little while ago, the shop's open till eleven every night now, and Jeff is shaving away to pay back that five hundred that Johnson, the livery man, sent to the Cubans, and –

Pathetic? tut! tut! You don't know Mariposa. Jeff has to work pretty late, but that's nothing – nothing at all, if you've worked hard all your lifetime. And Myra is back at the Telephone Exchange – they were glad enough to get her, and she says now that if there's one thing she hates, it's the stage, and she can't see how the actresses put up with it.

Anyway, things are not so bad. You see it was just at this time that Mr. Smith's caff opened, and Mr. Smith came to Jeff's Woman and said he wanted seven dozen eggs a day, and wanted them handy, and so the hens are back, and more of them, and they exult so every morning over the eggs they lay that if you wanted to talk of Rockefeller in the barber shop you couldn't hear his name for the cackling.

GOLGOTHA GINGHAM

# THE
# MARINE EXCURSION
## OF THE KNIGHTS
## OF PYTHIAS

**H**ALF-PAST SIX on a July morning! The Mariposa Belle is at the wharf, decked in flags, with steam up ready to start.

Excursion day!

Half-past six on a July morning, and Lake Wissanotti lying in the sun as calm as glass. The opal colours of the morning light are shot from the surface of the water.

Out on the lake the last thin threads of the mist are clearing away like flecks of cotton wool.

The long call of the loon echoes over the lake. The air is cool and fresh. There is in it all the new life of the land of the silent pine and the moving waters. Lake Wissanotti in the morning sunlight! Don't talk to me of the Italian lakes, or the Tyrol or the Swiss Alps. Take them away. Move them somewhere else. I don't want them.

Excursion Day, at half-past six of a summer morning! With the boat all decked in flags and all the people in Mariposa on the wharf, and the band in peaked caps with big cornets tied to their bodies ready to play at any minute! I say! Don't tell me about the Carnival of Venice and the

Delhi Durbar. Don't! I wouldn't look at them. I'd shut my eyes! For light and colour give me every time an excursion out of Mariposa down the lake to the Indian's Island out of sight in the morning mist. Talk of your Papal Zouaves and your Buckingham Palace Guard! I want to see the Mariposa band in uniform and the Mariposa Knights of Pythias with their aprons and their insignia and their picnic baskets and their five-cent cigars!

Half-past six in the morning, and all the crowd on the wharf and the boat due to leave in half an hour. Notice it! – in half an hour. Already she's whistled twice (at six, and at six fifteen), and at any minute now, Christie Johnson will step into the pilot house and pull the string for the warning whistle that the boat will leave in half an hour. So keep ready. Don't think of running back to Smith's Hotel for the sandwiches. Don't be fool enough to try to go up to the Greek Store, next to Netley's, and buy fruit. You'll be left behind for sure if you do. Never mind the sandwiches and the fruit! Anyway, here comes Mr. Smith himself with a huge basket of provender that would feed a factory. There must be sandwiches in that. I think I can hear them clinking. And behind Mr. Smith is the German waiter from the caff with another basket – indubitably lager beer; and behind him, the bar-tender of the hotel, carrying nothing, as far as one can see. But of course if you know Mariposa you will understand that why he looks so nonchalant and empty-handed is because he has two bottles of rye whiskey under his linen duster. You know, I think, the peculiar walk of a man with two bottles of whiskey in the inside pockets of a linen coat. In Mariposa, you see, to bring beer to an excursion is quite in keeping with public opinion. But, whiskey, – well, one has to be a little careful.

Do I say that Mr. Smith is here? Why, everybody's here. There's Hussell the editor of the Newspacket, wearing a blue ribbon on his coat, for the Mariposa Knights of Pythias are, by their constitution, dedicated to temperance; and there's Henry Mullins, the manager of the Exchange Bank, also a Knight of Pythias, with a small flask of Pogram's Special in his hip pocket as a sort of amendment to the constitution. And there's Dean Drone, the Chaplain of the Order, with a fishing-rod (you never saw such green bass as lie among the rocks at Indian's Island), and with a trolling line in case of maskinonge, and a landing net in case of pickerel, and with his eldest daughter, Lilian Drone, in case of young men. There never was such a fisherman as the Rev. Rupert Drone.

Perhaps I ought to explain that when I speak of the excursion as being of the Knights of Pythias, the thing must not be understood in any narrow sense. In Mariposa practically everybody belongs to the Knights of Pythias just as they do to everything else. That's the great thing about the town and that's what makes it so different from the city. Everybody is in everything.

You should see them on the seventeenth of March, for example, when everybody wears a green ribbon and they're all laughing and glad, – you know what the Celtic nature is, – and talking about Home Rule.

On St. Andrew's Day every man in town wears a thistle and shakes hands with everybody else, and you see the fine old Scotch honesty beaming out of their eyes.

And on St. George's Day! – well, there's no heartiness like the good old English spirit, after all; why shouldn't a man feel glad that he's an Englishman?

Then on the Fourth of July there are stars and stripes flying over half the stores in town, and suddenly all the men are seen to smoke cigars, and to know all about Roosevelt and Bryan and the Philippine Islands. Then you learn for the first time that Jeff Thorpe's people came from Massachusetts and that his uncle fought at Bunker Hill (it must have been Bunker Hill, – anyway Jefferson will swear it was in Dakota all right enough); and you find that George Duff has a married sister in Rochester and that her husband is all right; in fact, George was down there as recently as eight years ago. Oh, it's the most American town imaginable is Mariposa, – on the Fourth of July.

But wait, just wait, if you feel anxious about the solidity of the British connection, till the twelfth of the month, when everybody is wearing an orange streamer in his coat and the Orangemen (every man in town) walk in the big procession. Allegiance! Well, perhaps you remember the address they gave to the Prince of Wales on the platform of the Mariposa station as he went through on his tour to the west. I think that pretty well settled that question.

So you will easily understand that of course everybody belongs to the Knights of Pythias and the Masons and Oddfellows, just as they all belong to the Snow Shoe Club and the Girls' Friendly Society.

And meanwhile the whistle of the steamer has blown again for a quarter to seven: – loud and long this time, for any one not here now is late for certain; unless he should happen to come down in the last fifteen minutes.

What a crowd upon the wharf and how they pile on to the steamer! It's a wonder that the boat can hold them all. But that's just the marvellous thing about the Mariposa Belle.

I don't know, – I have never known, – where the steamers like the Mariposa Belle come from. Whether they are built by Harland and Wolff of Belfast, or whether, on the other hand, they are not built by Harland and Wolff of Belfast, is more than one would like to say offhand.

The Mariposa Belle always seems to me to have some of those strange properties that distinguish Mariposa itself. I mean, her size seems to vary so. If you see her there in the winter, frozen in the ice beside the wharf with a snowdrift against the windows of the pilot house, she looks a pathetic little thing the size of a butternut. But in the summer time, especially after you've been in Mariposa for a month or two, and have paddled alongside of her in a canoe, she gets larger and taller, and with a great sweep of black sides, till you see no difference between the Mariposa Belle and the Lusitania. Each one is a big steamer and that's all you can say.

Nor do her measurements help you much. She draws about eighteen inches forward, and more than that, – at least half an inch more, astern, and when she's loaded down with an excursion crowd she draws a good two inches more. And above the water, – why, look at all the decks on her! There's the deck you walk on to, from the wharf, all shut in, with windows along it, and the after cabin with the long table, and above that the deck with all the chairs piled upon it, and the deck in front where the band stands round in a circle, and the pilot house is higher than that, and above the pilot house is the board with the gold name and the flag pole and the steel ropes and the flags; and fixed in somewhere on the different levels is the lunch counter where they sell the sandwiches, and the engine room, and down below the deck level, beneath the water line, is the place where the crew sleeps. What with steps and stairs and passages and piles of cordwood for the engine, – oh no, I guess Harland and Wolff didn't build her. They couldn't have.

Yet even with a huge boat like the Mariposa Belle, it would be impossible for her to carry all of the crowd that you see in the boat and on the wharf. In reality, the crowd is made up of two classes, – all of the people in Mariposa who are going on the excursion and all those who are not. Some come for the one reason and some for the other.

The two tellers of the Exchange Bank are both there standing side by side. But one of them, – the one with the cameo pin and the long face like a horse, – is going, and the other, – with the other cameo pin and the face like another horse, – is not. In the same way, Hussell of the Newspacket is going, but his brother, beside him, isn't. Lilian Drone is going, but her sister can't; and so on all through the crowd.

And to think that things should look like that on the morning of a steamboat accident.

How strange life is!

To think of all these people so eager and anxious to catch the steamer, and some of them running to catch it, and so fearful that they might miss it, – the morning of a steamboat accident. And the captain blowing his whistle, and warning them so severely that he would leave them behind, – leave them out of the accident! And everybody crowding so eagerly to be in the accident.

Perhaps life is like that all through.

Strangest of all to think, in a case like this, of the people who were left behind, or in some way or other prevented from going, and always afterwards told of how they had escaped being on board the Mariposa Belle that day!

Some of the instances were certainly extraordinary.

Nivens, the lawyer, escaped from being there merely by the fact that he was away in the city.

Towers, the tailor, only escaped owing to the fact that, not intending to go on the excursion he had stayed in bed till eight o'clock and so had not gone. He narrated afterwards that waking up that morning at half-past five, he had thought of the excursion and for some unaccountable reason had felt glad that he was not going.

The case of Yodel, the auctioneer, was even more inscrutable. He had been to the Oddfellows' excursion on the train the week before and to the Conservative picnic the week before that, and had decided not to go on this trip. In fact, he had not the least intention of going. He narrated afterwards how the night before someone had stopped him on the corner of Nippewa and Tecumseh Streets (he indicated the very spot) and asked: "Are you going to take in the excursion to-morrow?" and he had said, just as simply as he was talking when narrating it: "No." And ten minutes after that, at the corner of Dalhousie and Brock Streets (he offered to lead a party of verification to the precise place) somebody else had stopped him and asked: "Well, are you going on the steamer trip to-morrow?" Again he had answered: "No," apparently almost in the same tone as before.

He said afterwards that when he heard the rumour of the accident it seemed like the finger of Providence, and fell on his knees in thankfulness.

There was the similar case of Morison (I mean the one in Glover's hardware store that married one of the Thompsons). He said afterwards that he had read so much in the papers about accidents lately, – mining accidents, and aeroplanes and gasoline, – that he had grown nervous. The night before his wife had asked him at supper: "Are you going on the excursion?" He had answered: "No, I don't think I feel like it," and had added: "Perhaps your mother might like to go." And the next evening just at dusk, when the news ran through the town, he said the first thought that flashed through his head was: "Mrs. Thompson's on that boat."

He told this right as I say it – without the least doubt or confusion. He never for a moment imagined she was on the Lusitania or the Olympic or any other boat. He knew she was on this one. He said you could have knocked him down where he stood. But no one had. Not even when he got halfway down, – on his knees, and it would have been easier still to knock him down or kick him. People do miss a lot of chances.

Still, as I say, neither Yodel nor Morison nor anyone thought about there being an accident until just after sundown when they –

Well, have you ever heard the long booming whistle of a steamboat two miles out on the lake in the dusk, and while you listen and count and wonder, seen the crimson rockets going up against the sky and then heard the fire bell ringing right there beside you in the town, and seen the people running to the town wharf?

That's what the people of Mariposa saw and felt that summer evening as they watched the Mackinaw life-boat go plunging out into the lake with seven sweeps to a side and the foam clear to the gunwale with the lifting stroke of fourteen men!

But, dear me, I am afraid that this is no way to tell a story. I suppose the true art would have been to have said nothing about the accident till it happened. But when you write about Mariposa, or hear of it, if you know the place, it's all so vivid and real that a thing like the contrast between the excursion crowd in the morning and the scene at night leaps into your mind and you must think of it.

But never mind about the accident, – let us turn back again to the morning.

The boat was due to leave at seven. There was no doubt about the hour, – not only seven, but seven sharp. The notice in the Newspacket said: "The boat will leave sharp at seven;" and the advertising posters on the telegraph poles on Missinaba Street that began "Ho, for Indian's Island!" ended up with the words: "Boat leaves at seven sharp." There was a big notice on the wharf that said: "Boat leaves sharp on time."

So at seven, right on the hour, the whistle blew loud and long, and then at seven fifteen three short peremptory blasts, and at seven thirty one quick angry call, – just one, – and very soon after that they cast off the last of the ropes and the Mariposa Belle sailed off in her cloud of flags, and the band of the Knights of Pythias, timing it to a nicety, broke into the "Maple Leaf for Ever!"

I suppose that all excursions when they start are much the same. Anyway, on the Mariposa Belle everybody went running up and down all over the boat with deck chairs and camp stools and baskets, and found places, splendid places to sit, and then got scared that there might be better ones and chased off again. People hunted for places out of the sun and when they got them swore that they weren't going to freeze to please anybody; and the people in the sun said that they hadn't paid fifty cents to be roasted. Others said that they hadn't paid fifty cents to get covered with cinders, and there were still others who hadn't paid fifty cents to get shaken to death with the propeller.

Still, it was all right presently. The people seemed to get sorted out into the places on the boat where they belonged. The women, the older ones, all gravitated into the cabin on the lower deck and by getting round the table with needlework, and with all the windows shut, they soon had it, as they said themselves, just like being at home.

All the young boys and the toughs and the men in the band got down on the lower deck forward, where the boat was dirtiest and where the anchor was and the coils of rope.

And upstairs on the after deck there were Lilian Drone and Miss Lawson, the high school teacher, with a book of German poetry, – Gothey I think it was, – and the bank teller and the younger men.

In the centre, standing beside the rail, were Dean Drone and Dr. Gallagher, looking through binocular glasses at the shore.

Up in front on the little deck forward of the pilot house was a group of the older men, Mullins and Duff and Mr. Smith in a deck chair, and beside him Mr. Golgotha Gingham, the undertaker of Mariposa, on a stool. It was part of Mr. Gingham's principles to take in an outing of this sort, a business matter, more or less, – for you never know what may happen at these water parties. At any rate, he was there in a neat suit of black, not, of course, his heavier or professional suit, but a soft clinging effect as of burnt paper that combined gaiety and decorum to a nicety.

"Yes," said Mr. Gingham, waving his black glove in a general way towards the shore, "I know the lake well, very well. I've been pretty much all over it in my time."

"Canoeing?" asked somebody.

"No," said Mr. Gingham, "not in a canoe." There seemed a peculiar and quiet meaning in his tone.

"Sailing, I suppose," said somebody else.

"No," said Mr. Gingham. "I don't understand it."

"I never knowed that you went on to the water at all, Gol," said Mr. Smith, breaking in.

"Ah, not now," explained Mr. Gingham; "it was years ago, the first summer I came to Mariposa. I was on the water practically all day. Nothing like it to give a man an appetite and keep him in shape."

"Was you camping?" asked Mr. Smith.

"We camped at night," assented the undertaker, "but we put in practically the whole day on the water. You see we were after a party that had come up here from the city on his vacation and gone out in a sailing canoe. We were dragging. We were up every morning at sunrise, lit a fire on the beach and cooked breakfast, and then we'd light our pipes and be off with the net for a whole day. It's a great life," concluded Mr. Gingham wistfully.

"Did you get him?" asked two or three together.

There was a pause before Mr. Gingham answered.

"We did," he said, – "down in the reeds past Horseshoe Point. But it was no use. He turned blue on me right away."

After which Mr. Gingham fell into such a deep reverie that the boat had steamed another half-mile down the lake before anybody broke the silence again.

Talk of this sort, – and after all what more suitable for a day on the water? – beguiled the way.

Down the lake, mile by mile over the calm water, steamed the Mariposa Belle. They passed Poplar Point where the high sand-banks are with all the swallows' nests in them, and Dean Drone and Dr. Gallagher looked at them alternately through the binocular glasses, and it was wonderful how plainly one could see the swallows and the banks and the shrubs, – just as plainly as with the naked eye.

And a little further down they passed the Shingle Beach, and Dr. Gallagher, who knew Canadian history, said to Dean Drone that it was strange to think that Champlain had landed there with his French explorers three hundred years ago; and Dean Drone, who didn't know Canadian history, said it was stranger still to think that the hand of the Almighty had piled up the hills and rocks long before that; and Dr. Gallagher said it was wonderful how the French had found their way through such a pathless wilderness; and Dean Drone said that it was wonderful also to think that the Almighty had placed even the smallest shrub in its appointed place. Dr. Gallagher said it filled him with admiration. Dean Drone said it filled him with awe. Dr. Gallagher said he'd been full of it ever since he was a boy; and Dean Drone said so had he.

Then a little further, as the Mariposa Belle steamed on down the lake, they passed the Old Indian Portage where the great grey rocks are; and Dr. Gallagher drew Dean Drone's attention to the place where the narrow canoe track wound up from the shore to the woods, and Dean Drone said he could see it perfectly well without the glasses.

Dr. Gallagher said that it was just here that a party of five hundred French had made their way with all their baggage and accoutrements across the rocks of the divide and down to the Great Bay. And Dean Drone said that it reminded him of Xenophon leading his ten thousand Greeks over the hill passes of Armenia down to the sea. Dr. Gallagher said that he had often wished he could have seen and spoken to Champlain, and Dean Drone said how much he regretted to have never known Xenophon.

And then after that they fell to talking of relics and traces of the past, and Dr. Gallagher said that if Dean Drone would come round to his house some night he would show him some Indian arrow heads that he had dug up in his garden. And Dean Drone said that if Dr. Gallagher would come round to the rectory any afternoon he would show him a map of Xerxes' invasion of Greece. Only he must come some time between the Infant Class and the Mothers' Auxiliary.

So presently they both knew that they were blocked out of one another's houses for some time to come, and Dr. Gallagher walked forward and told Mr. Smith, who had never studied Greek, about Champlain crossing the rock divide.

Mr. Smith turned his head and looked at the divide for half a second and then said he had crossed a worse one up north back of the Wahnipitae and that the flies were Hades, – and then went on playing freezeout poker with the two juniors in Duff's bank.

So Dr. Gallagher realized that that's always the way when you try to tell people things, and that as far as gratitude and appreciation goes one might as well never read books or travel anywhere or do anything.

In fact, it was at this very moment that he made up his mind to give the arrows to the Mariposa Mechanics' Institute, – they afterwards became, as you know, the Gallagher Collection. But, for the time being, the doctor was sick of them and wandered off round the boat and watched Henry Mullins showing George Duff how to make a John Collins without lemons, and finally went and sat down among the Mariposa band and wished that he hadn't come.

So the boat steamed on and the sun rose higher and higher, and the freshness of the morning changed into the full glare of noon, and they went on to where the lake began to narrow in at its foot, just where the Indian's Island is, – all grass and trees and with a log wharf running into the water. Below it the Lower Ossawippi runs out of the lake, and quite near are the rapids, and you can see down among the trees the red brick of the power house and hear the roar of the leaping water.

The Indian's Island itself is all covered with trees and tangled vines, and the water about it is so still that it's all reflected double and looks the same either way up. Then when the steamer's whistle blows as it comes into the wharf, you hear it echo among the trees of the island, and reverberate back from the shores of the lake.

The scene is all so quiet and still and unbroken, that Miss Cleghorn, – the sallow girl in the telephone exchange, that I spoke of – said she'd like to be buried there. But all the people were so busy getting their baskets and gathering up their things that no one had time to attend to it.

I mustn't even try to describe the landing and the boat crunching against the wooden wharf and all the people running to the same side of the deck and Christie Johnson calling out to the crowd to keep to the starboard and nobody being able to find it. Everyone who has been on a Mariposa excursion knows all about that.

Nor can I describe the day itself and the picnic under the trees. There were speeches afterwards, and Judge Pepperleigh gave such offence by bringing in Conservative politics that a man called Patriotus Canadiensis wrote and asked for some of the invaluable space of the Mariposa Times-Herald and exposed it.

I should say that there were races too, on the grass on the open side of the island, graded mostly according to ages, – races for boys under thirteen and girls over nineteen and all that sort of thing. Sports are generally conducted on that plan in Mariposa. It is realized that a woman of sixty has an unfair advantage over a mere child.

Dean Drone managed the races and decided the ages and gave out the prizes; the Wesleyan minister helped, and he and the young student, who was relieving in the Presbyterian Church, held the string at the winning point.

They had to get mostly clergymen for the races because all the men had wandered off, somehow, to where they were drinking lager beer out of two kegs stuck on pine logs among the trees.

But if you've ever been on a Mariposa excursion you know all about these details anyway.

So the day wore on and presently the sun came through the trees on a slant and the steamer whistle blew with a great puff of white steam and all the people came straggling down to the wharf and pretty soon the Mariposa Belle had floated out on to the lake again and headed for the town, twenty miles away.

I suppose you have often noticed the contrast there is between an excursion on its way out in the morning and what it looks like on the way home.

In the morning everybody is so restless and animated and moves to and fro all over the boat and asks questions. But coming home, as the afternoon gets later and the sun sinks beyond the hills, all the people seem to get so still and quiet and drowsy.

So it was with the people on the Mariposa Belle. They sat there on the benches and the deck chairs in little clusters, and listened to the regular beat of the propeller and almost dozed off asleep as they sat. Then when the sun set and the dusk drew on, it grew almost dark on the deck and so still that you could hardly tell there was anyone on board.

And if you had looked at the steamer from the shore or

from one of the islands, you'd have seen the row of lights from the cabin windows shining on the water and the red glare of the burning hemlock from the funnel, and you'd have heard the soft thud of the propeller miles away over the lake.

Now and then, too, you could have heard them singing on the steamer, – the voices of the girls and the men blended into unison by the distance, rising and falling in long-drawn melody: "O – Can-a-da – O – Can-a-da."

You may talk as you will about the intoning choirs of your European cathedrals, but the sound of "O Can-a-da," borne across the waters of a silent lake at evening is good enough for those of us who know Mariposa.

I think that it was just as they were singing like this: "O – Can-a-da," that word went round that the boat was sinking.

If you have ever been in any sudden emergency on the water, you will understand the strange psychology of it, – the way in which what is happening seems to become known all in a moment without a word being said. The news is transmitted from one to the other by some mysterious process.

At any rate, on the Mariposa Belle first one and then the other heard that the steamer was sinking. As far as I could ever learn the first of it was that George Duff, the bank manager, came very quietly to Dr. Gallagher and asked him if he thought that the boat was sinking. The doctor said no, that he had thought so earlier in the day but that he didn't now think that she was.

After that Duff, according to his own account, had said to Macartney, the lawyer, that the boat was sinking, and Macartney said that he doubted it very much.

Then somebody came to Judge Pepperleigh and woke him up and said that there was six inches of water in the steamer and that she was sinking. And Pepperleigh said it was perfect scandal and passed the news on to his wife and she said that they had no business to allow it and that if the steamer sank that was the last excursion she'd go on.

So the news went all round the boat and everywhere the people gathered in groups and talked about it in the angry and excited way that people have when a steamer is sinking on one of the lakes like Lake Wissanotti.

Dean Drone, of course, and some others were quieter about it, and said that one must make allowances and that naturally there were two sides to everything. But most of them wouldn't listen to reason at all. I think, perhaps, that some of them were frightened. You see the last time but one that the steamer had sunk, there had been a man drowned and it made them nervous.

What? Hadn't I explained about the depth of Lake Wissanotti? I had taken it for granted that you knew; and in any case parts of it are deep enough, though I don't suppose in this stretch of it from the big reed beds up to within a mile of the town wharf, you could find six feet of water in it if you tried. Oh, pshaw! I was not talking about a steamer sinking in the ocean and carrying down its screaming crowds of people into the hideous depths of green water. Oh, dear me no! That kind of thing never happens on Lake Wissanotti.

But what does happen is that the Mariposa Belle sinks every now and then, and sticks there on the bottom till they get things straightened up.

On the lakes round Mariposa, if a person arrives late anywhere and explains that the steamer sank, everybody understands the situation.

You see when Harland and Wolff built the Mariposa Belle, they left some cracks in between the timbers that you fill up with cotton waste every Sunday. If this is not attended to, the boat sinks. In fact, it is part of the law of the province that all the steamers like the Mariposa Belle must be properly corked, – I think that is the word, – every season. There are inspectors who visit all the hotels in the province to see that it is done.

So you can imagine now that I've explained it a little straighter, the indignation of the people when they knew that the boat had come uncorked and that they might be stuck out there on a shoal or a mud-bank half the night.

I don't say either that there wasn't any danger; anyway, it doesn't feel very safe when you realize that the boat is settling down with every hundred yards that she goes, and you look over the side and see only the black water in the gathering night.

Safe! I'm not sure now that I come to think of it that it isn't worse than sinking in the Atlantic. After all, in the Atlantic there is wireless telegraphy, and a lot of trained sailors and stewards. But out on Lake Wissanotti, – far out, so that you can only just see the lights of the town away off to the south, – when the propeller comes to a stop, – and you can hear the hiss of steam as they start to rake out the engine fires to prevent an explosion, – and when you turn from the red glare that comes from the furnace doors as they open them, to the black dark that is gathering over the lake, – and there's a night wind beginning to run among the rushes, – and you see the men going forward to the roof of the pilot house to send up the rockets to rouse the town, – safe? Safe yourself, if you like; as for me, let me once get back into Mariposa again, under the night shadow of the maple trees, and this shall be the last, last time I'll go on Lake Wissanotti.

Safe! Oh yes! Isn't it strange how safe other people's adventures seem after they happen? But you'd have been scared, too, if you'd been there just before the steamer sank, and seen them bringing up all the women on to the top deck.

I don't see how some of the people took it so calmly; how Mr. Smith, for instance, could have gone on smoking and telling how he'd had a steamer "sink on him" on Lake Nipissing and a still bigger one, a side-wheeler, sink on him in Lake Abbitibbi.

Then, quite suddenly, with a quiver, down she went. You could feel the boat sink, sink, – down, down, – would it never get to the bottom? The water came flush up to the lower deck, and then, – thank heaven, – the sinking stopped and there was the Mariposa Belle safe and tight on a reed bank.

Really, it made one positively laugh! It seemed so queer and, anyway, if a man has a sort of natural courage, danger makes him laugh. Danger! pshaw! fiddlesticks! everybody scouted the idea. Why, it is just the little things like this that give zest to a day on the water.

Within half a minute they were all running round looking for sandwiches and cracking jokes and talking of making coffee over the remains of the engine fires.

———

I don't need to tell at length how it all happened after that.

I suppose the people on the Mariposa Belle would have had to settle down there all night or till help came from the town, but some of the men who had gone forward and were peering out into the dark said that it couldn't be more than a mile across the water to Miller's Point. You could almost see it over there to the left, – some of them, I think, said "off on the port bow," because you know when you get mixed up in these marine disasters, you soon catch the atmosphere of the thing.

So pretty soon they had the davits swung out over the side and were lowering the old lifeboat from the top deck into the water.

There were men leaning out over the rail of the Mariposa Belle with lanterns that threw the light as they let her down, and the glare fell on the water and the reeds. But when they got the boat lowered, it looked such a frail, clumsy thing as one saw it from the rail above, that the cry was raised: "Women and children first!" For what was the sense, if it should turn out that the boat wouldn't even hold women and children, of trying to jam a lot of heavy men into it?

So they put in mostly women and children and the boat pushed out into the darkness so freighted down it would hardly float. In the bow of it was the Presbyterian student who was relieving the minister, and he called out that they were in the hands of Providence. But he was crouched and ready to spring out of them at the first moment.

So the boat went and was lost in the darkness except for the lantern in the bow that you could see bobbing on the water. Then presently it came back and they sent another load, till pretty soon the decks began to thin out and everybody got impatient to be gone.

It was about the time that the third boat-load put off that Mr. Smith took a bet with Mullins for twenty-five dollars, that he'd be home in Mariposa before the people in the boats had walked round the shore.

No one knew just what he meant, but pretty soon they saw Mr. Smith disappear down below into the lowest part of the steamer with a mallet in one hand and a big bundle of marline in the other.

They might have wondered more about it, but it was just at this time that they heard the shouts from the rescue boat – the big Mackinaw lifeboat – that had put out from the town with fourteen men at the sweeps when they saw the first rockets go up. I suppose there is always something inspiring about a rescue at sea, or on the water.

After all, the bravery of the lifeboat man is the true bravery, – expended to save life, not to destroy it.

Certainly they told for months after of how the rescue boat came out to the Mariposa Belle.

I suppose that when they put her in the water the lifeboat touched it for the first time since the old Macdonald Government placed her on Lake Wissanotti.

Anyway, the water poured in at every seam. But not for a moment, – even with two miles of water between them and the steamer, – did the rowers pause for that.

By the time they were half-way there the water was almost up to the thwarts, but they drove her on. Panting and exhausted (for mind you, if you haven't been in a fool boat like that for years, rowing takes it out of you), the rowers stuck to their task. They threw the ballast over and chucked into the water the heavy cork jackets and lifebelts that encumbered their movements. There was no thought of turning back. They were nearer to the steamer than the shore.

"Hang to it, boys," called the crowd from the steamer's deck, and hang they did.

They were almost exhausted when they got them; men leaning from the steamer threw them ropes and one by one every man was hauled aboard just as the lifeboat sank under their feet.

Saved! by Heaven, saved, by one of the smartest pieces of rescue work ever seen on the lake.

There's no use describing it; you need to see rescue work of this kind by lifeboats to understand it.

Nor were the lifeboat crew the only ones that distinguished themselves.

Boat after boat and canoe after canoe had put out from Mariposa to the help of the steamer. They got them all.

Pupkin, the other bank teller, with a face like a horse, who hadn't gone on the excursion, – as soon as he knew that the boat was signalling for help and that Miss Lawson was sending up rockets, – rushed for a row boat, grabbed an oar (two would have hampered him), and paddled madly out into the lake. He struck right out into the dark with the crazy skiff almost sinking beneath his feet. But they got him. They rescued him. They watched him, almost dead with exhaustion, make his way to the steamer, where he was hauled up with ropes. Saved! Saved!!

———

They might have gone on that way half the night, picking up the rescuers, only, at the very moment when the tenth load of people left for the shore, – just as suddenly and saucily as you please, up came the Mariposa Belle from the mud bottom and floated.

FLOATED?

Why, of course she did. If you take a hundred and fifty people off a steamer that has sunk, and if you get a man as shrewd as Mr. Smith to plug the timber seams with mallet and marline, and if you turn ten bandsmen of the Mariposa band on to your hand pump on the bow of the lower decks – float? why, what else can she do?

Then, if you stuff in hemlock into the embers of the fire that you were raking out, till it hums and crackles under the boiler, it won't be long before you hear the propeller thud – thudding at the stern again, and before the long roar of the steam whistle echoes over to the town.

And so the Mariposa Belle, with all steam up again and with the long train of sparks careering from the funnel, is heading for the town.

But no Christie Johnson at the wheel in the pilot house this time.

"Smith! Get Smith!" is the cry.

Can he take her in? Well, now! Ask a man who has had steamers sink on him in half the lakes from Temiscaming to the Bay, if he can take her in? Ask a man who has run a York boat down the rapids of the Moose when the ice is moving, if he can grip the steering wheel of the Mariposa Belle? So there she steams safe and sound to the town wharf!

Look at the lights and the crowd! If only the federal

census taker could count us now! Hear them calling and shouting back and forward from the deck to the shore! Listen! There is the rattle of the shore ropes as they get them ready, and there's the Mariposa band,    actually forming in a circle on the upper deck just as she docks, and the leader with his baton, – one – two – ready now, –

"O CAN-A-DA!"

**REVEREND DEAN DRONE**

# THE
# MINISTRATIONS OF
# THE REV. MR. DRONE

THE CHURCH OF ENGLAND in Mariposa is on a side
street, where the maple trees are thickest, a little up the hill
from the heart of the town. The trees above the church
and the grass plot that was once the cemetery, till they made
the new one (the Necropolis, over the brow of the hill), fill
out the whole corner. Down behind the church, with only
the driving shed and a lane between, is the rectory. It is a
little brick house with odd angles. There is a hedge and
a little gate, and a weeping ash tree with red berries.

At the side of the rectory, churchward, is a little
grass lawn with low hedges and at the side of that two
wild plum trees, that are practically always in white
blossom. Underneath them is a rustic table and chairs,
and it is here that you may see Rural Dean Drone, the
incumbent of the Church of England Church, sitting, in
the chequered light of the plum tress that is neither sun
nor shadow. Generally you will find him reading, and
when I tell you that at the end of the grass plot where the
hedge is highest there is a yellow bee hive with seven bees

that belong to Dean Drone, you will realize that it is only fitting that the Dean is reading in the Greek. For what better could a man be reading beneath the blossom of the plum trees, within the very sound of the bees, than the Pastorals of Theocritus? The light trash of modern romance might put a man to sleep in such a spot, but with such food for reflection as Theocritus, a man may safely close his eyes and muse on what he reads without fear of dropping into slumber.

Some men, I suppose, terminate their education when they leave their college. Not so Dean Drone. I have often heard him say that if he couldn't take a book in the Greek out on the lawn in a spare half-hour, he would feel lost. It's a certain activity of the brain that must be stilled somehow. The Dean, too, seemed to have a native feeling for the Greek language. I have often heard people who might sit with him on the lawn, ask him to translate some of it. But he always refused. One couldn't translate it, he said. It lost so much in the translation that it was better not to try. It was far wiser not to attempt it. If you undertook to translate it, there was something gone, something missing immediately. I believe that many classical scholars feel this way, and like to read the Greek just as it is, without the hazard of trying to put it into so poor a medium as English. So that when Dean Drone said that he simply couldn't translate it, I believe he was perfectly sincere.

Sometimes, indeed, he would read it aloud. That was another matter. Whenever, for example, Dr. Gallagher – I mean, of course, old Dr. Gallagher, not the young doctor (who was always out in the country in the afternoon) – would come over and bring his latest Indian relics to show to the Dean, the latter always read to him a passage or two. As soon as the doctor laid his tomahawk on the table, the Dean would reach for his Theocritus. I remember that on the day when Dr. Gallagher brought over the Indian skull that they had dug out of the railway embankment, and placed it on the rustic table, the Dean read to him so long from Theocritus that the doctor, I truly believe, dozed off in his chair. The Dean had to wait and fold his hands with the book across his knee, and close his eyes till the doctor should wake up again. And the skull was on the table between them, and from above the plum blossoms fluttered down, till they made flakes on it as white as Dr. Gallagher's hair.

I don't want you to suppose that the Rev. Mr. Drone spent the whole of his time under the trees. Not at all. In point of fact, the rector's life was one round of activity which he himself might deplore but was powerless to prevent. He had hardly sat down beneath the trees of an afternoon after his mid-day meal when there was the Infant Class at three, and after that, with scarcely an hour between, the Mothers' Auxiliary at five, and the next morning the Book Club, and that evening the Bible Study Class, and the next morning the Early Workers' Guild at eleven-thirty. The whole week was like that, and if one found time to sit down for an hour or so to recuperate it was the most one could do. After all, if a busy man spends the little bit of leisure that he gets in advanced classical study, there is surely no harm in it. I suppose, take it all in all, there wasn't a busier man than the Rural Dean among the Anglican clergy of the diocese.

If the Dean ever did snatch a half-day from his incessant work, he spent it in fishing. But not always that, for as likely as not, instead of taking a real holiday he would put in the whole afternoon amusing the children and the boys that he knew, by making kites and toys and clock-work steamboats for them.

It was fortunate for the Dean that he had the strange interest and aptitude for mechanical advices which he possessed, or otherwise this kind of thing would have been too cruel an imposition. But the Rev. Mr. Drone had a curious liking for machinery. I think I never heard him preach a better sermon than the one on Aeroplanes (Lo, what now see you on high Jeremiah Two).

So it was that he spent two whole days making a kite with Chinese wings for Teddy Moore, the photographer's son, and closed down the infant class for forty-eight hours so that Teddy Moore should not miss the pleasure of flying it, or rather seeing it flown. It is foolish to trust a Chinese kite to the hands of a young child.

In the same way the Dean made a mechanical top for little Marjorie Trewlaney, the cripple, to see spun: it would have been unwise to allow the afflicted girl to spin it. There was no end to the things that Mr. Drone could make, and always for the children. Even when he was making the sand-clock for poor little Willie Yodel (who died, you know) the Dean went right on with it and gave it to another child with just the same pleasure. Death, you know, to the clergy is a different thing from what it is to us. The Dean and Mr. Gingham used often to speak of it as they walked through the long grass of the new cemetery, the Necropolis. And when your Sunday walk is to your wife's grave, as the Dean's was, perhaps it seems different to anybody.

The Church of England Church, I said, stood close to the rectory, a tall, sweeping church, and inside a great reach of polished cedar beams that ran to the point of the roof. There used to stand on the same spot the little stone church that all the grown-up people in Mariposa still remember, a quaint little building in red and grey stone. About it was the old cemetery, but that was all smoothed out later into the grass plot round the new church, and the headstones laid out flat, and no new graves have been put there for ever so long. But the Mariposa children still walk round and read the headstones lying flat in the grass and look for the old ones, – because some of them are ever so old – forty or fifty years back.

Nor are you to think from all this that the Dean was not a man with serious perplexities. You could easily convince yourself of the contrary. For if you watched the Rev. Mr. Drone as he sat reading in the Greek, you would notice that no very long period ever passed without his taking up a sheet or two of paper that lay between the leaves of the Theocritus and that were covered close with figures.

And these the Dean would lay upon the rustic table, and he would add them up forwards and backwards, going first up the column and then down it to see that nothing had been left out, and then down it again to see what it was that must have been left out.

Mathematics, you will understand, were not the Dean's forte. They never were the forte of the men who had been trained at the little Anglican college with the clipped hedges and the cricket ground, where Rupert Drone had taken the gold medal in Greek fifty-two years ago. You will see the medal at any time lying there in its open box on the rectory table, in case of immediate need. Any of the Drone girls, Lilian, or Jocelyn, or Theodora, would show it to you. But, as I say, mathematics were not the rector's forte, and he blamed for it (in a Christian spirit, you will understand) the memory of his mathematical professor, and often he spoke with great bitterness. I have often heard him say that in his opinion the colleges ought to dismiss, of course in a Christian spirit, all the professors who are not, in the most reverential sense of the term, fit for their jobs.

No doubt many of the clergy of the diocese had suffered more or less just as the Dean had from lack of mathematical training. But the Dean always felt that his own case was especially to be lamented. For you see, if a man is trying to make a model aeroplane – for a poor family in the lower part of the town – and he is brought to a stop by the need of reckoning the coefficient of torsion of cast-iron rods, it shows plainly enough that the colleges are not truly filling their divine mission.

But the figures that I speak of were not those of the model aeroplane. These were far more serious. Night and day they had been with the rector now for the best part of ten years, and they grew, if anything, more intricate.

If, for example, you try to reckon the debt of a church – a large church with a great sweep of polished cedar beams inside, for the special glorification of the All Powerful, and with imported tiles on the roof for the greater glory of Heaven and with stained-glass windows for the exaltation of the All Seeing – if, I say, you try to reckon up the debt on such a church and figure out its interest and its present worth, less a fixed annual payment, it makes a pretty complicated sum. Then if you try to add to this the annual cost of insurance, and deduct from it three-quarters of a stipend, year by year, and then suddenly remember that three-quarters is too much, because you have forgotten the boarding-school fees of the littlest of the Drones (including French, as an extra – she must have it, all the older girls did), you have got a sum that pretty well defies ordinary arithmetic. The provoking part of it was that the Dean knew perfectly well that with the help of logarithms he could have done the thing in a moment. But at the Anglican college they had stopped short at that very place in the book. They had simply explained that Logos was a word and Arithmos a number, which at the time, seemed amply sufficient.

So the Dean was perpetually taking out his sheets of figures, and adding them upwards and downwards, and they never came the same. Very often Mr. Gingham, who was a warden, would come and sit beside the rector and ponder over the figures, and Mr. Drone would explain that with a book of logarithms you could work it out in a moment. You would simply open the book and run your finger up the columns (he illustrated exactly the way in which the finger was moved), and there you were. Mr. Gingham said that it was a caution, and that logarithms (I quote his exact phrase) must be a terror.

Very often, too, Nivens, the lawyer, who was a sidesman, and Mullins, the manager of the Exchange Bank, who was the chairman of the vestry, would come and take a look at the figures. But they never could make much of them, because the stipend part was not a matter that one could discuss.

Mullins would notice the item for a hundred dollars due on fire insurance and would say, as a business man, that surely that couldn't be fire insurance, and the Dean would say surely not, and change it: and Mullins would say surely there couldn't be fifty dollars for taxes, because there weren't any taxes, and the Dean would admit that of course it couldn't be for the taxes. In fact, the truth is that the Dean's figures were badly mixed, and the fault lay indubitably with the mathematical professor of two generations back.

It was always Mullins's intention some day to look into the finances of the church, the more so as his father had been with Dean Drone at the little Anglican college with the cricket ground. But he was a busy man. As he explained to the rector himself, the banking business nowadays is getting to be such that a banker can hardly call even his Sunday mornings his own. Certainly Henry Mullins could not. They belonged largely to Smith's Hotel, and during the fishing season they belonged away down the lake, so far away that practically no one, unless it was George Duff of the Commercial Bank, could see them.

But to think that all this trouble had come through the building of the new church.

That was the bitterness of it.

For the twenty-five years that Rural Dean Drone had preached in the little stone church, it had been his one aim, as he often put it in his sermons, to rear a larger Ark in Gideon. His one hope had been to set up a greater Evidence, or, very simply stated, to kindle a Brighter Beacon.

After twenty-five years of waiting, he had been able at last to kindle it. Everybody in Mariposa remembers the building of the church. First of all they had demolished the little stone church to make way for the newer Evidence. It seemed almost a sacrilege, as the Dean himself said, to lay hands on it. Indeed it was at first proposed to take the stone of it and build it into a Sunday School, as a lesser testimony. Then, when that provided impracticable, it was suggested that the stone be reverently fashioned into a wall that should stand as a token. And when even that could not be managed, the stone of the little church was laid reverently into a stone pile; afterwards it was devoutly sold to a building contractor, and, like so much else in life, was forgotten.

But the building of the church, no one, I think, will forget. The Dean threw himself into the work. With his coat off and his white shirt-sleeves conspicuous among the gang that were working at the foundations, he set his hand to the shovel, himself guided the road-scraper, urging on the horses, cheering and encouraging the men, till they begged him to desist. He mingled with the stone-masons, advising, helping, and giving counsel, till they pleaded with him to rest. He was among the carpenters, sawing, hammering, enquiring, suggesting, till they besought him to lay off. And he was night and day with the architect's assistants, drawing, planning, revising, till the architect told him to cut it out.

So great was his activity, that I doubt whether the new church would ever have been finished, had not the wardens and the vestry men insisted that Mr. Drone must take a holiday, and sent him on the Mackinaw trip up the lakes, – the only foreign travel of the Dean's life.

———

So in due time the New Church was built and it towered above the maple trees of Mariposa like a beacon on a hill. It stood so high that from the open steeple of it, where the bells were, you could see all the town lying at its feet, and the farmsteads to the south of it, and the railway like a double pencil line, and Lake Wissanotti spread out like a map. You could see and appreciate things from the height of the new church, – such as the size and the growing wealth of Mariposa, – that you never could have seen from the little stone church at all.

Presently the church was opened and the Dean preached his first sermon in it, and he called it a Greater Testimony, and he said that it was an earnest, or first fruit of endeavour, and that it was a token or pledge, and he named it also a covenant. He said, too, that it was an anchorage and a harbour and a lighthouse as well as being a city set upon a hill; and he ended by declaring it an Ark of Refuge and notified them that the Bible Class would meet in the basement of it on that and every other third Wednesday.

In the opening months of preaching about it the Dean had called the church so often an earnest and a pledge and a guerdon and a tabernacle, that I think he used to forget that it wasn't paid for. It was only when the agent of the building society and a representative of the Hosanna Pipe and Steam Organ Co. (Limited), used to call for quarterly payments that he was suddenly reminded of the fact. Always after these men came round the Dean used to preach a special sermon on sin, in the course of which he would mention that the ancient

Hebrews used to put unjust traders to death, – a thing of which he spoke with Christian serenity.

I don't think that at first anybody troubled much about the debt on the church. Dean Drone's figures showed that it was only a matter of time before it would be extinguished; only a little effort was needed, a little girding up of the loins of the congregation and they could shoulder the whole debt and trample it under their feet. Let them but set their hands to the plough and they could soon guide it into the deep water. Then they might furl their sails and sit every man under his own olive tree.

Meantime, while the congregation was waiting to gird up its loins, the interest on the debt was paid somehow, or, when it wasn't paid, was added to the principal.

I don't know whether you have had any experience with Greater Testimonies and with Beacons set on Hills. If you have, you will realize how, at first gradually, and then rapidly, their position from year to year grows more distressing. What with the building loan and the organ instalment, and the fire insurance, – a cruel charge, – and the heat and light, the rector began to realize as he added up the figures that nothing but logarithms could solve them. Then the time came when not only the rector, but all the wardens knew and the sidesmen knew that the debt was more than the church could carry; then the choir knew and the congregation knew and at last everybody knew; and there were special collections at Easter and special days of giving, and special weeks of tribulation, and special arrangements with the Hosanna Pipe and Steam Organ Co. And it was noticed that when the Rural Dean announced a service of Lenten Sorrow, – aimed more especially at the business men, – the congregation had diminished by forty per cent.

I suppose things are just the same elsewhere, – I mean the peculiar kind of discontent that crept into the Church of England congregation in Mariposa after the setting up of the Beacon. There were those who claimed that they had seen the error from the first, though they had kept quiet, as such people always do, from breadth of mind. There were those who had felt years before how it would end, but their lips were sealed from humility of spirit. What was worse was that there were others who grew dissatisfied with the whole conduct of the church.

Yodel, the auctioneer, for example, narrated how he had been to the city and had gone into a service of the Roman Catholic church: I believe, to state it more fairly, he had "dropped in," – the only recognized means of access to such a service. He claimed that the music that he had heard there was music, and that (outside of his profession) the chanting and intoning could not be touched.

Ed Moore, the photographer, also related that he had listened to a sermon in the city, and that if anyone would guarantee him a sermon like that he would defy you to keep him away from church. Meanwhile, failing the guarantee, he stayed away.

The very doctrines were impeached. Some of the congregation began to cast doubts on eternal punishment, – doubts so grave as to keep them absent from the Lenten Services of Sorrow. Indeed, Lawyer Macartney took up the whole question of the Athanasian Creed one afternoon with Joe Milligan, the dentist, and hardly left a clause of it intact.

All this time, you will understand, Dean Drone kept on with his special services, and leaflets, calls, and appeals went out from the Ark of Gideon like rockets from a sinking ship. More and more with every month the debt of the church lay heavy on his mind. At times he forgot it. At other times he woke up in the night and thought about it. Sometimes as he went down the street from the lighted precincts of the Greater Testimony and passed the Salvation Army, praying around a naphtha lamp under the open sky, it smote him to the heart with a stab.

But the congregation were wrong, I think, in imputing fault to the sermons of Dean Drone. There I do think they were wrong. I can speak from personal knowledge when I say that the rector's sermons were not only stimulating in matters of faith, but contained valuable material in regard to the Greek language, to modern machinery and to a variety of things that should have proved of the highest advantage to the congregation.

There was, I say, the Greek language. The Dean always showed the greatest delicacy of feeling in regard to any translation in or out of it that he made from the pulpit. He was never willing to accept even the faintest shade of rendering different from that commonly given without being assured of the full concurrence of the congregation. Either the translation must be unanimous and without contradiction, or he could not pass it. He would pause in his sermon and would say: "The original Greek is 'Hoson,' but perhaps you will allow me to translate it as equivalent to 'Hoyon.'" And they did. So that if there was any fault to be found it was purely on the side of the congregation for not entering a protest at the time.

It was the same way in regard to machinery. After all, what better illustrates the supreme purpose of the All Wise than such a thing as the dynamo or the reciprocating marine engine or the pictures in the Scientific American?

Then, too, if a man has had the opportunity to travel and has seen the great lakes spread out by the hand of Providence from where one leaves the new dock at the Sound to where one arrives safe and thankful with one's dear fellow-passengers in the spirit at the concrete landing stage at Mackinaw – is not this fit and proper material for the construction of an analogy or illustration? Indeed, even apart from an analogy, is it not mighty interesting to narrate, anyway? In any case, why should the church-wardens have sent the rector on the Mackinaw trip, if they had not expected him to make some little return for it?

I lay some stress on this point because the criticisms directed against the Mackinaw sermons always seemed so unfair. If the rector had described his experiences in the crude language of the ordinary newspaper, there might, I admit, have been something unfitting about it. But he was always careful to express himself in a way that showed, – or, listen, let me explain with an example.

"It happened to be my lot some years ago," he would say, "to find myself a voyager, just as one is a voyager on the sea of life, on the broad expanse of water which has been spread out to the north-west of us by the hand of Providence, at a height of five hundred and eighty-one feet above the level of the sea, – I refer, I may say, to Lake Huron."

Now, how different that is from saying: "I'll never forget the time I went on the Mackinaw trip." The whole thing has a different sound entirely. In the same way the Dean would go on:

"I was voyaging on one of those magnificent leviathans of the water, – I refer to the boats of the Northern Navigation Company, – and was standing beside the forward rail talking with a dear brother in the faith who was journeying westward also – I may say he was a commercial traveller, – and beside us was a dear sister in the spirit seated in a deck chair, while near us were two other dear souls in grace engaged in Christian pastime on the deck, – I allude more particularly to the game of deck billiards."

I leave it to any reasonable man whether, with that complete and fair-minded explanation of the environment, it was not perfectly proper to close down the analogy, as the rector did, with the simple words: "In fact, it was an extremely fine morning."

Yet there were some people, even in Mariposa, that took exception and spent their Sunday dinner time in making out that they couldn't understand what Dean Drone was talking about, and asking one another if they knew. Once, as he passed out from the doors of the Greater Testimony, the rector heard some one say: "The Church would be all right if that old mugwump was out of the pulpit." It went to his heart like a barbed thorn, and stayed there.

You know, perhaps, how a remark of that sort can stay and rankle, and make you wish you could hear it again to make sure of it, because perhaps you didn't hear it aright, and it was a mistake after all. Perhaps no one said it, anyway. You ought to have written it down at the time. I have seen the Dean take down the encyclopaedia in the rectory, and move his finger slowly down the pages of the letter M, looking for mugwump. But it wasn't there. I have known him, in his little study upstairs, turn over the pages of the "Animals of Palestine," looking for a mugwump. But there was none there. It must have been unknown in the greater days of Judea.

So things went on from month to month, and from year to year, and the debt and the charges loomed like a dark and gathering cloud on the horizon. I don't mean to say that efforts were not made to face the difficulty and to fight it. They were. Time after time the workers of the congregation got together and thought out plans for the extinction of the debt. But somehow, after every trial, the debt grew larger with each year, and every system that could be devised turned out more hopeless than the last.

They began, I think, with the "endless chain" of letters of appeal. You may remember the device, for it was all-popular in clerical circles some ten or fifteen years ago. You got a number of people to write each of them three letters asking for ten cents from three each of their friends and asking each of them to send on three similar letters. Three each from three each, and three each more from each! Do you observe the wonderful ingenuity of it? Nobody, I think, has forgotten how the Willing Workers of the Church of England Church of Mariposa sat down in the vestry room in the basement with a pile of stationery three feet high, sending out the letters. Some, I know, will never forget it. Certainly not Mr. Pupkin, the teller in the Exchange Bank, for it was here that he met Zena Pepperleigh, the judge's daughter, for the first time; and they worked so busily that they wrote out ever so many letters – eight or nine – in a single afternoon, and they discovered that their handwritings were awfully alike, which was one of the most extraordinary and amazing coincidences, you will admit, in the history of chirography.

But the scheme failed – failed utterly. I don't know why. The letters went out and were copied, broadcast and recopied, till you could see the Mariposa endless chain winding its way towards the Rocky Mountains. But they never got the ten cents. The Willing Workers wrote for it in thousands, but by some odd chance they never struck the person who had it.

Then after that there came a regular winter of effort. First of all they had a bazaar that was got up by the Girls' Auxiliary and held in the basement of the church. All the girls wore special costumes that were brought up from the city, and they had booths, where there was every imaginable thing for sale – pincushion covers, and chair covers, and sofa covers, everything that you can think of. If the people had once started buying them, the debt would have been lifted in no time. Even as it was the bazaar only lost twenty dollars.

After that, I think, was the magic lantern lecture that Dean Drone gave on "Italy and her Invaders." They got the lantern and the slides up from the city, and it was simply splendid. Some of the slides were perhaps a little confusing, but it was all there, – the pictures of the dense Italian jungle and the crocodiles and the naked invaders with their invading clubs. It was a pity that it was such a bad night, snowing hard, and a curling match on, or they would have made a lot of money out of the lecture. As it was the loss, apart from the breaking of the lantern, which was unavoidable, was quite trifling.

I can hardly remember all the things that there were after that. I recollect that it was always Mullins who arranged about renting the hall and printing the tickets and all that sort of thing. His father, you remember, had been at the Anglican college with Dean Drone, and though the rector was thirty-seven years older than Mullins, he leaned upon him, in matters of business, as upon a staff; and though Mullins was thirty-seven years younger than the Dean, he leaned against him, in matters of doctrine, as against a rock.

At one time they got the idea that what the public wanted was not anything instructive but something light and amusing. Mullins said that people loved to laugh. He said that if you get a lot of people all together and get them laughing you can do anything you like with them. Once they start to laugh they are lost. So they got Mr. Dreery, the English Literature teacher at the high school, to give an evening of readings from the Great Humorists from Chaucer to Adam Smith. They came mighty near to making a barrel of money out of that. If the people had once started laughing it would have been all over with them. As it was I heard a lot of them say that they simply wanted to scream with laughter: they said they just felt like bursting into peals of laughter all the time. Even when, in the more subtle parts, they didn't

MR. DREERY

feel like bursting out laughing, they said they had all they could do to keep from smiling. They said they never had such a hard struggle in their lives not to smile.

In fact the chairman said when he put the vote of thanks that he was sure if people had known what the lecture was to be like there would have been a much better "turn-out." But you see all that the people had to go on was just the announcement of the name of the lecturer, Mr. Dreery, and that he would lecture on English Humour All Seats Twenty-five Cents. As the chairman expressed it himself, if the people had had any idea, any idea at all, of what the lecture would be like they would have been there in hundreds. But how could they get an idea that it would be so amusing with practically nothing to go upon?

After that attempt things seemed to go from bad to worse. Nearly everybody was disheartened about it. What would have happened to the debt, or whether they would have ever paid it off, is more than I can say, if it hadn't occurred that light broke in on Mullins in the strangest and most surprising way you can imagine. It happened that he went away for his bank holidays, and while he was away he happened to be present in one of the big cities and saw how they went at it there to raise money. He came home in such a state of excitement that he went straight up from the Mariposa station to the rectory, valise and all, and he burst in one April evening to where the Rural Dean was sitting with the three girls beside the lamp in the front room, and he cried out:

"Mr. Drone, I've got it, – I've got a way that will clear the debt before you're a fortnight older. We'll have a Whirlwind Campaign in Mariposa!"

But stay! The change from the depth of depression to the pinnacle of hope is too abrupt. I must pause and tell you in another chapter of the Whirlwind Campaign in Mariposa.

PETE GLOVER

# THE
# WHIRLWIND
# CAMPAIGN
# IN MARIPOSA

IT WAS MULLINS, the banker, who told Mariposa all about the plan of a Whirlwind Campaign and explained how it was to be done. He'd happened to be in one of the big cities when they were raising money by a Whirlwind Campaign for one of the universities, and he saw it all.

He said he would never forget the scene on the last day of it, when the announcement was made that the total of the money raised was even more than what was needed. It was a splendid sight, – the business men of the town all cheering and laughing and shaking hands, and the professors with the tears streaming down their faces, and the Deans of the Faculties, who had given money themselves, sobbing aloud.

He said it was the most moving thing he ever saw.

So, as I said, Henry Mullins, who had seen it, explained to the others how it was done. He said that first of all a few of the business men got together quietly, – very quietly, indeed the more quietly the better, – and talked things over. Perhaps one of them would dine, – just quietly, – with another one and discuss the situation. Then these two would invite a third man, – possibly even a fourth, – to have lunch with them and talk in a general way, – even talk of other things part of the time. And so on in this way things would be discussed and looked at in different lights and viewed from different angles and then when everything was ready they would go at things with a rush. A central committee would be formed and sub-committees, with captains of each group and recorders and secretaries, and on a stated day the Whirlwind Campaign would begin.

Each day the crowd would all agree to meet at some stated place and eat lunch together, – say at a restaurant or at a club or at some eating place. This would go on every day with the interest getting keener and keener, and everybody getting more and more excited, till presently the chairman would announce that the campaign had succeeded and there would be the kind of scene that Mullins had described.

So that was the plan that they set in motion in Mariposa.

I don't wish to say too much about the Whirlwind Campaign itself. I don't mean to say that it was a failure. On the contrary, in many ways it couldn't have been a greater success, and yet somehow it didn't seem to work out just as Henry Mullins had said it would. It may be that there are differences between Mariposa and the larger cities that one doesn't appreciate at first sight. Perhaps it would have been better to try some other plan.

Yet they followed along the usual line of things

closely enough. They began with the regular system of some of the business men getting together in a quiet way.

First of all, for example, Henry Mullins came over quietly to Duff's rooms, over the Commercial Bank, with a bottle of rye whiskey, and they talked things over. And the night after that George Duff came over quietly to Mullins's rooms, over the Exchange Bank, with a bottle of Scotch whiskey. A few evenings after that Mullins and Duff went together, in a very unostentatious way, with perhaps a couple of bottles of rye, to Pete Glover's room over the hardware store. And then all three of them went up one night with Ed Moore, the photographer, to Judge Pepperleigh's house under pretence of having a game of poker. The very day after that, Mullins and Duff and Ed Moore, and Pete Glover and the judge got Will Harrison, the harness maker, to go out without any formality on the lake on the pretext of fishing. And the next night after that Duff and Mullins and Ed Moore and Pete Glover and Pepperleigh and Will Harrison got Alf Trelawney, the post-master, to come over, just in a casual way, to the Mariposa House, after the night mail, and the next day Mullins and Duff and –

But, pshaw! you see at once how the thing is worked. There's no need to follow that part of the Whirlwind Campaign further. But it just shows the power of organization.

And all this time, mind you, they were talking things over, and looking at things first in one light and then in another light, – in fact, just doing as the big city men do when there's an important thing like this under way.

So after things had been got pretty well into shape in this way, Duff asked Mullins one night, straight out, if he would be chairman of the Central Committee. He sprung it on him and Mullins had no time to refuse, but he put it to Duff straight whether he would be treasurer. And Duff had no time to refuse.

That gave things a start, and within a week they had the whole organization on foot. There was the Grand Central Committee and six groups or sub-committees of twenty men each, and a captain for every group. They had it all arranged on the lines most likely to be effective.

In one group there were all the bankers, Mullins and Duff and Pupkin (with the cameo pin), and about four others. They had their photographs taken at Ed Moore's studio, taken in a line with a background of icebergs – a winter scene – and a pretty penetrating crowd they looked, I can tell you. After all, you know, if you get a crowd of representative bank men together in any financial deal, you've got a pretty considerable leverage right away.

In the second group were the lawyers, Nivens and Macartney and the rest – about as level-headed a lot as you'd see anywhere. Get the lawyers of a town with you on a thing like this and you'll find you've got a sort of brain power with you that you'd never get without them.

Then there were the business men – there was a solid crowd for you, – Harrison, the harness maker, and Glover, the hardware man, and all that gang, not talkers, perhaps, but solid men who can tell you to a nicety how many cents there are in a dollar. It's all right to talk about education and that sort of thing, but if you want driving power and efficiency, get business men. They're seeing it every day in the city, and it's just the same in Mariposa. Why, in the big concerns in the city, if they found out a man was educated, they wouldn't have him, – wouldn't keep him there a minute. That's why the business men have to conceal it so much.

Then in the other teams there were the doctors and the newspaper men and the professional men like Judge Pepperleigh and Yodel the auctioneer.

It was all organized so that every team had its head-quarters, two of them in each of the three hotels – one upstairs and one down. And it was arranged that there would be a big lunch every day, to be held in Smith's caff, round the corner of Smith's Northern Health Resort and Home of the Wissanotti Angler, – you know the place. The lunch was divided up into tables, with a captain for each table to see about things to drink, and of course all the tables were in competition with one another. In fact the competition was the very life of the whole thing.

It's just wonderful how these things run when they're organized. Take the first luncheon, for example. There they all were, every man in his place, every captain at his post at the top of the table. It was hard, perhaps, for some of them to get there. They had very likely to be in their stores and banks and offices till the last minute and then make a dash for it. It was the cleanest piece of teamwork you ever saw.

You have noticed already, I am sure, that a good many of the captains and committee men didn't belong to the

The WHIRLWIND CAMPAIGN
GRAND CENTRAL COMMITTEE

Church of England Church. Glover, for instance, was a Presbyterian, till they ran the picket fence of the manse two feet on to his property, and after that he became a freethinker. But in Mariposa, as I have said, everybody likes to be in everything and naturally a Whirlwind Campaign was a novelty. Anyway it would have been a poor business to keep a man out of the lunches merely on account of his religion. I trust that the day for that kind of religious bigotry is past.

Of course the excitement was when Henry Mullins at the head of the table began reading out the telegrams and letters and messages. First of all there was a telegram of good wishes from the Anglican Lord Bishop of the Diocese to Henry Mullins and calling him Dear Brother in Grace – the Mariposa telegraph office is a little unreliable and it read: "Dear Brother in grease," but that was good enough. The Bishop said that his most earnest wishes were with them.

Then Mullins read a letter from the Mayor of Mariposa – Pete Glover was mayor that year – stating that his keenest desires were with them: and then one from the Carriage Company saying that its heartiest good will was all theirs; and then one from the Meat Works saying that its nearest thoughts were next to them. Then he read one from himself, as head of the Exchange Bank, you understand, informing him that he had heard of his project and assuring him of his liveliest interest in what he proposed.

At each of these telegrams and messages there was round after round of applause, so that you could hardly hear yourself speak or give an order. But that was nothing to when Mullins got up again, and beat on the table for silence and made one of those crackling speeches – just the way business men speak – the kind of speech that a college man simply can't make. I wish I could repeat it all. I remember that it began: "Now boys, you know what we're here for, gentlemen," and it went on just as good as that all through.

When Mullins had done he took out a fountain pen and wrote out a cheque for a hundred dollars, conditional on the fund reaching fifty thousand. And there was a burst of cheers all over the room.

Just the moment he had done it, up sprang George Duff, – you know the keen competition there is, as a straight matter of business, between the banks in Mariposa, – up sprang George Duff, I say, and wrote out a cheque for another hundred conditional on the fund reaching seventy thousand. You never heard such cheering in your life.

And then when Netley walked up to the head of the table and laid down a cheque for a hundred dollars conditional on the fund reaching one hundred thousand the room was in an uproar. A hundred thousand dollars! Just think of it! The figures fairly stagger one. To think of a hundred thousand dollars raised in five minutes in a little place like Mariposa!

And even that was nothing! In less than no time there was such a crowd round Mullins trying to borrow his pen all at once that his waistcoat was all stained with ink. Finally when they got order at last, and Mullins stood up and announced that the conditional fund had reached a quarter of a million, the whole place was a perfect babel of cheering. Oh, these Whirlwind Campaigns are wonderful things!

I can tell you the Committee felt pretty proud that first day. There was Henry Mullins looking a little bit flushed and excited, with his white waistcoat and an American Beauty rose, and with ink marks all over him from the cheque signing; and he kept telling them that he'd known all along that all that was needed was to get the thing started and telling again about what he'd seen at the University Campaign and about the professors crying, and wondering if the high school teachers would come down for the last day of the meetings.

Looking back on the Mariposa Whirlwind, I can never feel that it was a failure. After all, there is a sympathy and a brotherhood in these things when men work shoulder to shoulder. If you had seen the canvassers of the Committee going round the town that evening shoulder to shoulder from the Mariposa House to the Continental and up to Mullins's rooms and over to Duff's, shoulder to shoulder, you'd have understood it.

I don't say that every lunch was quite such a success as the first. It's not always easy to get out of the store if you're a busy man, and a good many of the Whirlwind Committee found that they had just time to hurry down and snatch their lunch and get back again. Still, they came, and snatched it. As long as the lunches lasted, they came. Even if they had simply to rush it and grab something to eat and drink without time to talk to anybody, they came.

No, no, it was not lack of enthusiasm that killed the

Whirlwind Campaign in Mariposa. It must have been something else. I don't just know what it was but I think it had something to do with the financial, the book-keeping side of the thing.

It may have been, too, that the organization was not quite correctly planned. You see, if practically everybody is on the committees, it is awfully hard to try to find men to canvass, and it is not allowable for the captains and the committee men to canvass one another, because their gifts are spontaneous. So the only thing that the different groups could do was to wait round in some likely place – say the bar parlour of Smith's Hotel – in the hope that somebody might come in who could be canvassed.

You might ask why they didn't canvass Mr. Smith himself, but of course they had done that at the very start, as I should have said. Mr. Smith had given them two hundred dollars in cash conditional on the lunches being held in the caff of his hotel; and it's awfully hard to get a proper lunch – I mean the kind to which a Bishop can express regret at not being there – under a dollar twenty-five. So Mr. Smith got back his own money, and the crowd began eating into the benefactions, and it got more and more complicated whether to hold another lunch in the hope of breaking even, or to stop the campaign.

It was disappointing, yes. In spite of all the success and the sympathy, it was disappointing. I don't say it didn't do good. No doubt a lot of the men got to know one another better than ever they had before. I have myself heard Judge Pepperleigh say that after the campaign he knew all of Pete Glover that he wanted to. There was a lot of that kind of complete satiety. The real trouble about the Whirlwind Campaign was that they never clearly understood which of them were the whirlwind and who were to be the campaign.

Some of them, I believe, took it pretty much to heart. I know that Henry Mullins did. You could see it. The first day he came down to the lunch, all dressed up with the American Beauty and the white waistcoat. The second day he only wore a pink carnation and a grey waistcoat. The third day he had on a dead daffodil and a cardigan undervest, and on the last day, when the high school teachers should have been there, he only wore his office suit and he hadn't even shaved. He looked beaten.

It was that night that he went up to the rectory to tell the news to Dean Drone. It had been arranged, you know, that the rector should not attend the lunches, so as to let the whole thing come as a surprise; so that all he knew about it was just scraps of information about the crowds at the lunch and how they cheered and all that. Once, I believe, he caught sight of the Newspacket with a two-inch headline: A QUARTER OF A MILLION, but he wouldn't let himself read further because it would have spoilt the surprise.

I saw Mullins, as I say, go up the street on his way to Dean Drone's. It was middle April and there was ragged snow on the streets, and the nights were dark still, and cold. I saw Mullins grit his teeth as he walked, and I know that he held in his coat pocket his own cheque for the hundred, with the condition taken off it, and he said that there were so many skunks in Mariposa that a man might as well be in the Head Office in the city.

The Dean came out to the little gate in the dark, – you could see the lamplight behind him from the open door of the rectory, – and he shook hands with Mullins and they went in together.

HENRY MULLINS

# THE
# BEACON ON THE HILL

**M**ULLINS SAID AFTERWARD that it was ever so much easier than he thought it would have been. The Dean, he said, was so quiet. Of course if Mr. Drone had started to swear at Mullins, or tried to strike him, it would have been much harder. But as it was he was so quiet that part of the time he hardly seemed to follow what Mullins was saying. So Mullins was glad of that, because it proved that the Dean wasn't feeling disappointed as, in a way, he might have.

Indeed, the only time when the rector seemed animated and excited in the whole interview was when Mullins said that the campaign had been ruined by a lot of confounded mugwumps. Straight away the Dean asked if those mugwumps had really prejudiced the outcome of the campaign. Mullins said there was no doubt of it, and the Dean enquired if the presence of mugwumps was fatal in matters of endeavour, and Mullins said that it was. Then the rector asked if even one mugwump was, in the Christian sense, deleterious. Mullins said that one mugwump would kill anything. After that the Dean hardly spoke at all.

In fact, the rector presently said that he mustn't detain Mullins too long and that he had detained him too long already and that Mullins must be weary from his train journey and that in cases of extreme weariness nothing but a sound sleep was of any avail; he himself, unfortunately, would not be able to avail himself of the priceless boon of slumber until he had first retired to his study to write some letters; so that Mullins, who had a certain kind of social quickness of intuition, saw that it was time to leave, and went away.

It was midnight as he went down the street, and a dark, still night. That can be stated positively because it came out in court afterwards. Mullins swore that it was a dark night; he admitted, under examination, that there may have been the stars, or at least some of the less important of them, though he had made no attempt, as brought out on cross-examination, to count them: there may have been, too, the electric lights, and Mullins was not willing to deny that it was quite possible that there was more or less moonlight. But that there was no light that night in the form of sunlight, Mullins was absolutely certain. All that, I say, came out in court.

But meanwhile the rector had gone upstairs to his study and had seated himself in front of his table to write his letters. It was here always that he wrote his sermons. From the window of the room you looked through the bare white maple trees to the sweeping outlines of the church shadowed against the night sky, and beyond that, though far off, was the new cemetery where the rector walked of a Sunday (I think I told you why): beyond that again, for the window faced the east, there lay, at no very great distance, the New Jerusalem. There were no better things that a man might look towards from his study window, nor anything that could serve as a better aid to writing.

But this night the Dean's letters must have been difficult indeed to write. For he sat beside the table holding his pen and with his head bent upon his other hand, and though he sometimes put a line or two on the paper, for the most part he sat motionless. The fact is that Dean Drone was not trying to write letters, but only one letter. He was writing a letter of resignation. If you have not done that for forty years it is extremely difficult to get the words.

So at least the Dean found it. First he wrote one set of words and then he sat and thought and wrote something else. But nothing seemed to suit.

The real truth was that Dean Drone, perhaps more than he knew himself, had a fine taste for words and effects, and when you feel that a situation is entirely out of the common, you naturally try, if you have that instinct, to give it the right sort of expression.

I believe that at the time when Rupert Drone had taken the medal in Greek over fifty years ago, it was only a twist of fate that had prevented him from becoming a great writer. There was a buried author in him just as there was a buried financier in Jefferson Thorpe. In fact, there were many people in Mariposa like that, and for all I know you may yourself have seen such elsewhere. For instance, I am certain that Billy Rawson, the telegraph operator at Mariposa, could easily have invented radium. In the same way one has only to read the advertisements of Mr. Gingham, the undertaker, to know that there is still in him a poet, who could have written on death far more attractive verses than the Thanatopsis of Cullen Bryant, and under a title less likely to offend the public and drive away custom. He has told me this himself.

So the Dean tried first this and then that and nothing would seem to suit. First of all he wrote:

"It is now forty years since I came among you, a youth full of life and hope and ardent in the work before me –" Then he paused, doubtful of the accuracy and clearness of the expression, read it over again and again in deep thought and then began again:

"It is now forty years since I came among you, a broken and melancholy boy, without life or hope, desiring only to devote to the service of this parish such few years as might remain of an existence blighted before it had truly begun –" And then again the Dean stopped. He read what he had written; he frowned; he crossed it through with his pen. This was no way to write, this thin egotistical strain of complaint. Once more he started:

"It is now forty years since I came among you, a man already tempered and trained, except possibly in mathematics –" And then again the rector paused and his mind drifted away to the memory of the Anglican professor that I spoke of, who had had so little sense of his higher mission as to omit the teaching of logarithms. And the rector mused so long that when he began again it seemed to him that it was simpler and better to discard the personal note altogether, and he wrote:

"There are times, gentlemen, in the life of a parish, when it comes to an epoch which brings it to a moment when it reaches a point –"

The Dean stuck fast again, but refusing this time to be beaten went resolutely on:

"– reaches a point where the circumstances of the moment make the epoch such as to focus the life of the parish in that time."

Then the Dean saw that he was beaten, and he knew that he not only couldn't manage the parish but couldn't say so in proper English, and of the two the last was the bitterer discovery.

He raised his head, and looked for a moment through the window at the shadow of the church against the night, so outlined that you could almost fancy that the light of the New Jerusalem was beyond it. Then he wrote, and this time not to the world at large but only to Mullins:

"My dear Harry, I want to resign my charge. Will you come over and help me?"

When the Dean at last rose from writing that, I think it was far on in the night. As he rose he looked again through the window, looked once and then once more, and so stood with widening eyes, and his face set towards what he saw.

What was that? That light in the sky there, eastward? – near or far he could not say. Was it already the dawn of the New Jerusalem brightening in the east, or was it – look – in the church itself, – what is that? – that dull red glow that shines behind the stained-glass windows, turning them to crimson? that fork of flame that breaks now from the casement and flashes upward, along the wood – and see – that sudden sheet of fire that springs the windows of the church with the roar of splintered glass and surges upward into the sky, till the dark night and the bare trees and sleeping street of Mariposa are all illumined with its glow!

Fire! Fire! and the sudden sound of the bell now, breaking upon the night.

So stood the Dean erect, with one hand pressed against the table for support, while the Mariposa fire bell struck out its warning to the sleeping town, – stood there while the street grew loud with the tumult of voices, – with the roaring gallop of the fire brigade, – with the harsh note of the gong – and over all other sounds, the great seething of the flames that tore their way into the beams and rafters of the pointed church and flared above it like a torch into the midnight sky.

So stood the Dean, and as the church broke thus into a very beacon kindled upon a hill, – sank forward without a sign, his face against the table, stricken.

You need to see a fire in a place such as Mariposa, a town still half of wood, to know what fire means. In the city it is all different. To the onlooker, at any rate, a fire is only a spectacle, nothing more. Everything is arranged, organized, certain. It is only once perhaps in a century that fire comes to a large city as it comes to the little wooden town like Mariposa as a great Terror of the Night.

That, at any rate, is what it meant in Mariposa that night in April, the night the Church of England Church burnt down. Had the fire gained but a hundred feet, or less, it could have reached from the driving shed behind the church to the backs of the wooden shops of the Main Street, and once there not all the waters of Lake Wissanotti could stay the course of its destruction. It was for that hundred feet that they fought, the men of Mariposa, from the midnight call of the bell till the slow coming of the day.

They fought the fire, not to save the church, for that was doomed from the first outbreak of the flames, but to stop the spread of it and save the town. They fought it at the windows, and at the blazing doors, and through the yawning furnace of the open belfry; fought it, with the Mariposa engine thumping and panting in the street, itself aglow with fire like a servant demon fighting its own kind, with tall ladders reaching to the very roof, and with hoses that poured their streams of tossing water foaming into the flames.

Most of all they fought to save the wooden driving shed behind the church from which the fire could leap into the heart of Mariposa. That was where the real fight was, for the life of the town. I wish you could have seen how they turned the hose against the shingles, ripping and tearing them from their places with the force of the driven water: how they mounted on the roof, axe in hand, and cut madly at the rafters to bring the building down, while the black clouds of smoke rolled in volumes about the men as they worked. You could see the fire horses harnessed with logging chains to the uprights of the shed to tear the building from its place.

Most of all I wish you could have seen Mr. Smith, proprietor, as I think you know, of Smith's Hotel, there on the roof with a fireman's helmet on, cutting through the main beam of solid cedar, twelve by twelve, that held tight still when the rafters and the roof tree were down already, the shed on fire in a dozen places, and the other men driven from the work by the flaming sparks, and by the

MARIPOSA VOLUNTEER
FIRE BRIGADE

strangle of the smoke. Not so Mr. Smith! See him there as he plants himself firm at the angle of the beams, and with the full impact of his two hundred and eighty pounds drives his axe into the wood! I tell you it takes a man from the pine country of the north to handle an axe! Right, left, left, right, down it comes, with never a pause or stay, never missing by a fraction of an inch the line of the stroke! At it, Smith! Down with it! Till with a shout from the crowd the beam gapes asunder, and Mr. Smith is on the ground again, roaring his directions to the men and horses as they haul down the shed, in a voice that dominates the fire itself.

Who made Mr. Smith the head and chief of the Mariposa fire brigade that night, I cannot say. I do not know even where he got the huge red helmet that he wore, nor had I ever heard till the night the church burnt down that Mr. Smith was a member of the fire brigade at all. But it's always that way. Your little narrow-chested men may plan and organize, but when there is something to be done, something real, then it's the man of size and weight that steps to the front every time. Look at Bismarck and Mr. Gladstone and President Taft and Mr. Smith, – the same thing in each case.

I suppose it was perfectly natural that just as soon as Mr. Smith came on the scene he put on somebody's helmet and shouted his directions to the men and bossed the Mariposa fire brigade like Bismarck with the German parliament.

The fire had broken out late, late at night, and they fought it till the day. The flame of it lit up the town and the bare grey maple trees, and you could see in the light of it the broad sheet of the frozen lake, snow covered still.

It kindled such a beacon as it burned that from the other side of the lake the people on the night express from the north could see it twenty miles away. It lit up such a testimony of flame that Mariposa has never seen the like of it before or since. Then when the roof crashed in and the tall steeple tottered and fell, so swift a darkness seemed to come that the grey trees and the frozen lake vanished in a moment as if blotted out of existence.

When the morning came the great church of Mariposa was nothing but a ragged group of walls with a sodden heap of bricks and blackened wood, still hissing here and there beneath the hose with the sullen anger of a conquered fire.

Round the ruins of the fire walked the people of Mariposa next morning, and they pointed out where the wreck of the steeple had fallen, and where the bells of the church lay in a molten heap among the bricks, and they talked of the loss that it was and how many dollars it would take to rebuild the church, and whether it was insured and for how much. And there were at least fourteen people who had seen the fire first, and more than that who had given the first alarm, and ever so many who knew how fires of this sort could be prevented.

Most noticeable of all you could see the sidesmen and the wardens and Mullins, the chairman of the vestry, talking in little groups about the fire. Later in the day there came from the city the insurance men and the fire appraisers, and they too walked about the ruins, and talked with the wardens and the vestry men. There was such a luxury of excitement in the town that day that it was just as good as a public holiday.

But the strangest part of it was the unexpected sequel. I don't know through what error of the Dean's figures it happened, through what lack of mathematical training the thing turned out as it did. No doubt the memory of the mathematical professor was heavily to blame for it, but the solid fact is that the Church of England Church of Mariposa turned out to be insured for a hundred thousand, and there were the receipts and the vouchers, all signed and regular, just as they found them in a drawer of the rector's study. There was no doubt about it. The insurance people might protest as they liked. The straight, plain fact was that the church was insured for about twice the whole amount of the cost and the debt and the rector's salary and the boarding-school fees of the littlest of the Drones all put together.

There was a Whirlwind Campaign for you! Talk of raising money, – that was something like! I wonder if the universities and the city institutions that go round trying to raise money by the slow and painful method called a Whirlwind Campaign, that takes perhaps all day to raise fifty thousand dollars, ever thought of anything so beautifully simple as this.

The Greater Testimony that had lain so heavily on the congregation went flaming to its end, and burned up its debts and its obligations and enriched its worshippers by its destruction. Talk of a beacon on a hill! You can hardly beat that one.

I wish you could have seen how the wardens and the sidesmen and Mullins, the chairman of the vestry, smiled and chuckled at the thought of it. Hadn't they said all along that all that was needed was a little faith and effort? And here it was, just as they said, and they'd been right after all.

Protest from the insurance people? Legal proceedings to prevent payment? My dear sir! I see you know nothing about the Mariposa court, in spite of the fact that I have already said that it was one of the most precise instruments of British fair play ever established. Why, Judge Pepperleigh disposed of the case and dismissed the protest of the company in less than fifteen minutes! Just what the jurisdiction of Judge Pepperleigh's court is I don't know, but I do know that in upholding the rights of a Christian congregation – I am quoting here the text of the decision – against the intrigues of a set of infernal skunks that make too much money anyway, the Mariposa court is without an equal. Pepperleigh even threatened the plaintiffs with the penitentiary, or worse.

How the fire started no one ever knew. There was a queer story that went about to the effect that Mr. Smith and Mr. Gingham's assistant had been seen very late that night carrying an automobile can of kerosene up the street. But that was amply disproved by the proceedings of the court, and by the evidence of Mr. Smith himself. He took his dying oath, – not his ordinary one as used in the License cases, but his dying one, – that he had not carried a can of kerosene up the street, and that anyway it was the rottenest kind of kerosene he had ever seen and no more use than so much molasses. So that point was settled.

Dean Drone? Did he get well again? Why, what makes you ask that? You mean, was his head at all affected after the stroke? No, it was not. Absolutely not. It was not affected in the least, though how anybody who knows him now in Mariposa could have the faintest idea that his mind was in any way impaired by the stroke is more than I can tell. The engaging of Mr. Uttermost, the curate, whom perhaps you have heard preach in the new church, had nothing whatever to do with Dean Drone's head. It was merely a case of the pressure of overwork. It was felt very generally by the wardens that, in these days of specialization, the rector was covering too wide a field, and that if he should abandon some of the lesser duties of his office, he might devote his energies more intently to the Infant Class. That was all. You may hear him there any afternoon, talking to them, if you will stand under the maple trees and listen through the open windows of the new Infant School.

And, as for audiences, for intelligence, for attention – well, if I want to find listeners who can hear and understand about the great spaces of Lake Huron, let me tell of it, every time face to face with the blue eyes of the Infant Class, fresh from the infinity of spaces greater still. Talk of grown-up people all you like, but for listeners let me have the Infant Class with their pinafores and their Teddy Bears and their feet not even touching the floor, and Mr. Uttermost may preach to his heart's content of the newer forms of doubt revealed by the higher criticism.

So you will understand that the Dean's mind is, if anything, even keener, and his head even clearer than before. And if you want proof of it, notice him there beneath the plum blossoms reading in the Greek: he has told me that he finds that he can read, with the greatest ease, works in the Greek that seemed difficult before. Because his head is so clear now.

And sometimes, – when his head is very clear, – as he sits there reading beneath the plum blossoms he can hear them singing beyond, and his wife's voice.

PETER
PUPKIN

# THE
# EXTRAORDINARY
# ENTANGLEMENT OF
# MR. PUPKIN

JUDGE PEPPERLEIGH lived in a big house with hardwood floors and a wide piazza that looked over the lake from the top of Oneida Street.

Every day about half-past five he used to come home from his office in the Mariposa Court House. On some days as he got near the house he would call out to his wife:

"Almighty Moses, Martha! who left the sprinkler on the grass?"

On other days he would call to her from quite a little distance off: "Hullo, mother! Got any supper for a hungry man?"

And Mrs. Pepperleigh never knew which it would be.

On the days when he swore at the sprinkler you could see his spectacles flash like dynamite. But on the days when he called: "Hullo, mother," they were simply irradiated with kindliness.

Some days, I say, he would cry out with a perfect whine of indignation: "Suffering Caesar! has that infernal dog torn up those geraniums again?" And other days you would hear him singing out: "Hullo, Rover! Well, doggie, well, old fellow!"

In the same way at breakfast, the judge, as he looked over the morning paper, would sometimes leap to his feet with a perfect howl of suffering, and cry: "Everlasting Moses! the Liberals have carried East Elgin." Or else he would lean back from the breakfast table with the most good-humoured laugh you ever heard and say: "Ha! ha! the Conservatives have carried South Norfolk."

And yet he was perfectly logical, when you come to think of it. After all, what is more annoying to a sensitive, highly-strung man than an infernal sprinkler playing all over the place, and what more agreeable to a good-natured, even-tempered fellow than a well-prepared supper? Or, what is more likeable than one's good, old, affectionate dog bounding down the path from sheer delight at seeing you, – or more execrable than an infernal whelp that has torn up the geraniums and is too old to keep, anyway?

As for politics, well, it all seemed reasonable enough. When the Conservatives got in anywhere, Pepperleigh laughed and enjoyed it, simply because it does one good to see a straight, fine, honest fight where the best man wins. When a Liberal got in, it made him mad, and he said so, – not, mind you, from any political bias, for his office forbid it, – but simply because one can't bear to see the country go absolutely to the devil.

I suppose, too, it was partly the effect of sitting in court all day listening to cases. One gets what you might call the judicial temper of mind. Pepperleigh had it so strongly developed that I've seen him kick a hydrangea pot to pieces with his foot because the accursed thing wouldn't flower. He once threw the canary cage clear into the lilac bushes because the "blasted bird wouldn't stop singing." It was a straight case of judicial temper. Lots of judges have it, developed in just the same broad, all-round way as with Judge Pepperleigh.

I think it must be passing sentences that does it. Anyway, Pepperleigh had the aptitude for passing sentences so highly perfected that he spent his whole time at it inside of court and out. I've heard him hand out sentences for the Sultan of Turkey and Mrs. Pankhurst and the Emperor of Germany that made one's blood run cold. He would sit there on the piazza of a summer evening reading the paper, with dynamite sparks flying from his spectacles as he sentenced the Czar of Russia to ten years in the salt mines – and made it fifteen a few minutes afterwards. Pepperleigh always read the foreign news – the news of things that he couldn't alter – as a form of wild and stimulating torment.

So you can imagine that in some ways the judge's house was a pretty difficult house to go to. I mean you can see how awfully hard it must have been for Mr. Pupkin. I tell you it took some nerve to step up on that piazza and say, in a perfectly natural, off-hand way: "Oh, how do you do, judge? Is Miss Zena in? No, I won't stay, thanks; I think I ought to be going. I simply called." A man who can do that has got to have a pretty fair amount of savoir what do you call it, and he's got to be mighty well shaved and have his cameo pin put in his tie at a pretty undeniable angle before he can tackle it. Yes, and even then he may need to hang round behind the lilac bushes for half an hour first, and cool off. And he's apt to make pretty good time down Oneida Street on the way back.

Still, that's what you call love, and if you've got it, and are well shaved, and your boots well blacked, you can do things that seem almost impossible. Yes, you can do anything, even if you do trip over the dog in getting off the piazza.

Don't suppose for a moment that Judge Pepperleigh was an unapproachable or a harsh man always and to everybody. Even Mr. Pupkin had to admit that that couldn't be so. To know that, you had only to see Zena Pepperleigh put her arm round his neck and call him Daddy. She would do that even when there were two or three young men sitting on the edge of the piazza. You know, I think, the way they sit on the edge in Mariposa. It is meant to indicate what part of the family they have come to see. Thus when George Duff, the bank manager, came up to the Pepperleigh house, he always sat in a chair on the verandah and talked to the judge. But when Pupkin or Mallory Tompkins or any fellow like that came, he sat down in a sidelong fashion on the edge of the boards and then they knew exactly what he was there for. If he knew the house well, he leaned his back against the verandah post and smoked a cigarette. But that took nerve.

But I am afraid that this is a digression, and, of course, you know all about it just as well as I do. All that I was trying to say was that I don't suppose that the judge had ever spoken a cross word to Zena in his life. – Oh, he threw her novel over the grape-vine, I don't deny that, but then why on earth should a girl read trash like the *Errant Quest of the Palladin Pilgrim*, and the *Life of Sir Galahad*, when the house was full of good reading like *The Life of Sir John A. Macdonald*, and *Pioneer Days in Tecumseh Township*?

Still, what I mean is that the judge never spoke harshly to Zena, except perhaps under extreme provocation; and I am quite sure that he never, never had to Neil. But then what father ever would want to speak angrily to such a boy as Neil Pepperleigh? The judge took no credit himself for that; the finest grown boy in the whole county and so broad and big that they took him into the Missinaba Horse when he was only seventeen. And clever, – so clever that he didn't need to study; so clever that he used to come out at the foot of the class in mathematics at the Mariposa high school through sheer surplus of brain power. I've heard the judge explain it a dozen times. Why, Neil was so clever that he used to be able to play billiards at the Mariposa House all evening when the other boys had to stay at home and study.

Such a powerful looking fellow, too! Everybody in Mariposa remembers how Neil Pepperleigh smashed in the face of Peter McGinnis, the Liberal organizer, at the big election – you recall it – when the old Macdonald Government went out. Judge Pepperleigh had to try him for it the next morning – his own son. They say there never was such a scene even in the Mariposa court. There was, I believe, something like it on a smaller scale in Roman history, but it wasn't half as dramatic. I remember Judge Pepperleigh leaning forward to pass the sentence, – for a judge is bound, you know, by his oath, – and how grave he looked and yet so proud and happy, like a man doing his duty and sustained by it, and he said:

"My boy, you are innocent. You smashed in Peter McGinnis's face, but you did it without criminal intent. You put a face on him, by Jehoshaphat! that he won't lose for six months, but you did it without evil purpose or malign design. My boy, look up! Give me your hand! You leave this court without a stain upon your name."

They said it was one of the most moving scenes ever enacted in the Mariposa Court.

But the strangest thing is that if the judge had known what every one else in Mariposa knew, it would have broken his heart. If he could have seen Neil with the drunken flush on his face in the billiard room of the Mariposa House, – if he had known, as every one else did, that Neil was crazed with drink the night he struck the Liberal organizer when the old Macdonald Government went out, – if he could have known that even on that last day Neil was drunk when he rode with the Missinaba Horse to the station to join the Third Contingent for the war, and all the street of the little town was one great roar of people –

But the judge never knew, and now he never will. For if you could find it in the meanness of your soul to tell him, it would serve no purpose now except to break his heart, and there would rise up to rebuke you the pictured vision of an untended grave somewhere in the great silences of South Africa.

Did I say above, or seem to imply, that the judge sometimes spoke harshly to his wife? Or did you gather for a minute that her lot was one to lament over or feel sorry for? If so, it just shows that you know nothing about such things, and that marriage, at least as it exists in Mariposa, is a sealed book to you. You are as ignorant as Miss Spiffkins, the biology teacher at the high school, who always says how sorry she is for Mrs. Pepperleigh. You get that impression simply because the judge howled like an Algonquin Indian when he saw the sprinkler running on the lawn. But are you sure you know the other side of it? Are you quite sure when you talk like Miss Spiffkins does about the rights of it, that you are taking all things into account? You might have thought differently perhaps of the Pepperleighs, anyway, if you had been there that evening when the judge came home to his wife with one hand pressed to his temple and in the other the cablegram that said that Neil had been killed in action in South Africa. That night they sat together with her hand in his, just as they had sat together thirty years ago when he was a law student in the city.

Go and tell Miss Spiffkins that! Hydrangeas, – canaries, – temper, – blazes! What does Miss Spiffkins know about it all?

But in any case, if you tried to tell Judge Pepperleigh about Neil now he wouldn't believe it. He'd laugh it to scorn. That is Neil's picture, in uniform, hanging in the dining-room beside the Fathers of Confederation. That military-looking man in the picture beside him is General Kitchener, whom you may perhaps have heard of, for he was very highly spoken of in Neil's letters. All round the room, in fact, and still more in the judge's library upstairs, you will see pictures of South Africa and the departure of the Canadians (there are none of the return), and of Mounted Infantry and of Unmounted Cavalry and a lot of things that only soldiers and the fathers of soldiers know about.

So you can realize that for a fellow who isn't military, and who wears nothing nearer to a uniform than a daffodil tennis blazer, the judge's house is a devil of a house to come to.

I think you remember young Mr. Pupkin, do you not? I have referred to him several times already as the junior teller in the Exchange Bank. But if you know Mariposa at all you have often seen him. You have noticed him, I am sure, going for the bank mail in the morning in an office suit effect of clinging grey with a gold necktie pin shaped like a riding whip. You have seen him often enough going down to the lake front after supper, in tennis things, smoking a cigarette and with a paddle and a crimson canoe cushion under his arm. You have seen him entering Dean Drone's church in a top hat and a long frock coat nearly to his feet. You have seen him, perhaps, playing poker in Peter Glover's room over the hardware store and trying to look as if he didn't hold three aces, – in fact, giving absolutely no sign of it beyond the wild flush in his face and the fact that his hair stands on end.

That kind of reticence is a thing you simply have to learn in banking. I mean, if you've got to be in a position where you know for a fact that the Mariposa Packing Company's account is overdrawn by sixty-four dollars, and yet daren't say anything about it, not even to the girls that you play tennis with, – I don't say, not a casual hint as a reference, but not really tell them, not, for instance, bring down the bank ledger to the tennis court and show them, – you learn a sort of reticence and self-control that people outside of banking circles never can attain.

Why, I've known Pupkin at the Fireman's Ball lean

NEIL
PEPPERLEIGH

against the wall in his dress suit and talk away to Jim Eliot, the druggist, without giving the faintest hint or indication that Eliot's note for twenty-seven dollars had been protested that very morning. Not a hint of it. I don't say he didn't mention it, in a sort of way, in the supper room, just to one or two, but I mean there was nothing in the way he leant up against the wall to suggest it.

But, however, I don't mention that as either for or against Mr. Pupkin. That sort of thing is merely the A B C of banking, as he himself told me when explaining why it was that he hesitated to divulge the exact standing of the Mariposa Carriage Company. Of course, once you get past the A B C you can learn a lot that is mighty interesting.

So I think that if you know Mariposa and understand even the rudiments of banking, you are perfectly acquainted with Mr. Pupkin. What? You remember him as being in love with Miss Lawson, the high school teacher? In love with HER? What a ridiculous idea. You mean merely because on the night when the Mariposa Belle sank with every soul on board, Pupkin put off from the town in a skiff to rescue Miss Lawson. Oh, but you're quite wrong. That wasn't LOVE. I've heard Pupkin explain it himself a dozen times. That sort of thing, – paddling out to a sinking steamer at night in a crazy skiff, – may indicate a sort of attraction, but not real love, not what Pupkin came to feel afterwards. Indeed, when he began to think of it, it wasn't even attraction, it was merely respect, – that's all it was. And anyway, that was long before, six or seven months back, and Pupkin admitted that at the time he was a mere boy.

———

Mr. Pupkin, I must explain, lived with Mallory Tompkins in rooms over the Exchange Bank, on the very top floor, the third, with Mullins's own rooms below them. Extremely comfortable quarters they were, with two bedrooms and a sitting-room that was all fixed up with snowshoes and tennis rackets on the walls and dance programmes and canoe club badges and all that sort of thing.

Mallory Tompkins was a young man with long legs and check trousers who worked on the Mariposa Times-Herald. That was what gave him his literary taste. He used to read Ibsen and that other Dutch author – Bumstone Bumstone, isn't it? – and you can judge that he was a mighty intellectual fellow. He was so intellectual that he was, as he himself admitted, a complete eggnostic. He and Pupkin used to have the most tremendous arguments about creation and evolution, and how if you study at a school of applied science you learn that there's no hell beyond the present life.

Mallory Tompkins used to prove absolutely that the miracles were only electricity, and Pupkin used to admit that it was an awfully good argument, but claimed that he had heard it awfully well answered in a sermon, though unfortunately he had forgotten how.

Tompkins used to show that the flood was contrary to geology, and Pupkin would acknowledge that the point was an excellent one, but that he had read a book, – the title of which he ought to have written down, – which explained geology away altogether.

Mallory Tompkins generally got the best of the merely logical side of the arguments, but Pupkin – who was a tremendous Christian – was much stronger in the things he had forgotten. So the discussions often lasted till far into the night, and Mr. Pupkin would fall asleep and dream of a splendid argument, which would have settled the whole controversy, only unfortunately he couldn't recall it in the morning.

Of course, Pupkin would never have thought of considering himself on an intellectual par with Mallory Tompkins. That would have been ridiculous. Mallory Tompkins had read all sorts of things and had half a mind to write a novel himself – either that or a play. All he needed, he said, was to have a chance to get away somewhere by himself and think. Every time he went away to the city Pupkin expected that he might return with the novel all finished; but though he often came back with his eyes red from thinking, the novel as yet remained incomplete.

Meantime, Mallory Tompkins, as I say, was a mighty intellectual fellow. You could see that from the books on the bamboo bookshelves in the sitting-room. There was, for instance, the "Encyclopaedia Metropolitana" in forty volumes, that he bought on the instalment plan for two dollars a month. Then when they took that away, there was the "History of Civilization," in fifty volumes at fifty cents a week for fifty years. Tompkins had read in it half-way through the Stone Age before they took it from him. After that there was the "Lives of the Painters," one volume at a time – a splendid thing in which you could read all about Aahrens, and Aachenthal, and Aax and men of that class. After all, there's nothing like educating oneself. Mallory Tompkins knew about the opening period of all sorts of things, and in regard to people whose names began with "A" you couldn't stick him.

I don't mean that he and Mr. Pupkin lived a mere routine of studious evenings. That would be untrue. Quite often their time was spent in much less commendable ways than that, and there were poker parties in their sitting-room that didn't break up till nearly midnight. Card-playing, after all, is a slow business, unless you put money on it, and, besides, if you are in a bank and are handling money all day, gambling has a fascination.

I've seen Pupkin and Mallory Tompkins and Joe Milligan, the dentist, and Mitchell the ticket agent, and the other "boys" sitting round the table with matches enough piled up in front of them to stock a factory. Ten matches counted for one chip and ten chips made a cent – so you see they weren't merely playing for the fun of the thing. Of course it's a hollow pleasure. You realize that when you wake up at night parched with thirst, ten thousand matches to the bad. But banking is a wild life and everybody knows it.

Sometimes Pupkin would swear off and keep away from the cursed thing for weeks, and then perhaps he'd see by sheer accident a pile of matches on the table, or a match lying on the floor and it would start the craze in him. I am using his own words – a "craze" – that's what he called it when he told Miss Lawson all about it, and she promised to cure him of it. She would have, too. Only, as I say, Pupkin found that what he had mistaken for attraction was only respect. And there's no use worrying a woman that you respect about your crazes.

———

It was from Mallory Tompkins that Pupkin learned all about the Mariposa people, because Pupkin came from away off – somewhere down in the Maritime Provinces – and didn't know a soul. Mallory Tompkins used to tell him about Judge Pepperleigh, and what a wonderfully clever man he was and how he would have been in the Supreme Court for certain if the Conservative Government had stayed in another fifteen or twenty years instead of coming to a premature end. He used to talk so much about the Pepperleighs, that Pupkin was sick of the very name. But just as soon as he had seen Zena Pepperleigh he couldn't hear enough of them. He would have talked with Tompkins for hours about the judge's dog Rover. And as for Zena, if he could have brought her name over his lips, he would have talked of her forever.

He first saw her – by one of the strangest coincidences in the world – on the Main Street of Mariposa. If he hadn't happened to be going up the street and she to be coming down it, the thing wouldn't have happened. Afterwards they both admitted that it was one of the most peculiar coincidences they ever heard of. Pupkin owned that he had had the strangest feeling that morning as if something were going to happen – a feeling not at all to be classed with the one of which he had once spoken to Miss Lawson, and which was, at the most, a mere anticipation of respect.

But, as I say, Pupkin met Zena Pepperleigh on the twenty-sixth of June, at twenty-five minutes to eleven. And at once the whole world changed. The past was all blotted out. Even in the new forty volume edition of the "Instalment Record of Humanity" that Mallory Tompkins had just received – Pupkin wouldn't have bothered with it.

She – that word henceforth meant Zena – had just come back from her boarding-school, and of all times of year coming back from a boarding-school and for wearing a white shirt waist and a crimson tie and for carrying a tennis racket on the stricken street of a town – commend me to the month of June in Mariposa.

And, for Pupkin, straight away the whole town was irradiated with sunshine, and there was such a singing of the birds, and such a dancing of the rippled waters of the lake, and such a kindliness in the faces of all the people, that only those who have lived in Mariposa, and been young there, can know at all what he felt.

The simple fact is that just the moment he saw Zena Pepperleigh, Mr. Pupkin was clean, plumb, straight, flat, absolutely in love with her.

Which fact is so important that it would be folly not to close the chapter and think about it.

ZENA
PEPPERLEIGH

# THE
# FORE-ORDAINED ATTACHMENT OF ZENA PEPPERLEIGH AND PETER PUPKIN

ZENA PEPPERLEIGH used to sit reading novels on the piazza of the judge's house, half hidden by the Virginia creepers. At times the book would fall upon her lap and there was such a look of unstilled yearning in her violet eyes that it did not entirely disappear even when she picked up the apple that lay beside her and took another bite out of it.

With hands clasped she would sit there dreaming all the beautiful day-dreams of girlhood. When you saw that faraway look in her eyes, it meant that she was dreaming that a plumed and armoured knight was rescuing her from the embattled keep of a castle beside the Danube. At other times she was being borne away by an Algerian corsair over the blue waters of the Mediterranean and was reaching out her arms towards France to say farewell to it.

Sometimes when you noticed a sweet look of resignation that seemed to rest upon her features, it meant that Lord Ronald de Chevereux was kneeling at her feet, and that she was telling him to rise, that her humbler birth must ever be a bar to their happiness, and Lord Ronald was getting into an awful state about it, as English peers do at the least suggestion of anything of the sort.

Or, if it wasn't that, then her lover had just returned to her side, tall and soldierly and sunburned, after fighting for ten years in the Soudan for her sake, and had come back to ask her for her answer and to tell her that for ten years her face had been with him even in the watches of the night. He was asking her for a sign, any kind of sign, – ten years in the Soudan entitles them to a sign, – and Zena was plucking a white rose, just one, from her hair, when she would hear her father's step on the piazza and make a grab for the *Pioneers of Tecumseh Township*, and start reading it like mad.

She was always, as I say, being rescued and being borne away, and being parted, and reaching out her arms to France and to Spain, and saying good-bye forever to Valladolid or the old grey towers of Hohenbranntwein.

And I don't mean that she was in the least exceptional or romantic, because all the girls in Mariposa were just like that. An Algerian corsair could have come into the town and had a dozen of them for the asking, and as for a wounded English officer, – well, perhaps it's better not to talk about it outside or the little town would become a regular military hospital.

Because, mind you, the Mariposa girls are all right. You've only to look at them to realize that. You see, you can get in Mariposa a print dress of pale blue or pale pink for a dollar twenty that looks infinitely better than anything you ever see in the city, – especially if you can wear with it a broad straw hat and a background of maple trees and the green grass of a tennis court. And if you remember, too, that these are cultivated girls who have all been to the Mariposa high school and can do decimal fractions, you will understand that an Algerian corsair would sharpen his scimitar at the very sight of them.

Don't think either that they are all dying to get married; because they are not. I don't say they wouldn't take an errant knight, or a buccaneer or a Hungarian refugee, but for the ordinary marriages of ordinary people they feel nothing but a pitying disdain. So it is that each one of them in due time marries an enchanted prince and goes to live in one of the little enchanted houses in the lower part of the town.

I don't know whether you know it, but you can rent an enchanted house in Mariposa for eight dollars a month, and some of the most completely enchanted are the cheapest. As for the enchanted princes, they find them in the strangest places, where you never expected to see them, working – under a spell, you understand, – in drug-stores and printing offices, and even selling things in shops. But to be able to find them you have first to read ever so many novels about Sir Galahad and the Errant Quest and that sort of thing.

Naturally then Zena Pepperleigh, as she sat on the piazza, dreamed of bandits and of wounded officers and of Lord Ronalds riding on foam-flecked chargers. But that she ever dreamed of a junior bank teller in a daffodil blazer riding past on a bicycle, is pretty hard to imagine. So, when Mr. Pupkin came tearing past up the slope of Oneida Street at a speed that proved that he wasn't riding there merely to pass the house, I don't suppose that Zena Pepperleigh was aware of his existence.

That may be a slight exaggeration. She knew, perhaps, that he was the new junior teller in the Exchange Bank and that he came from the Maritime Provinces, and that nobody knew who his people were, and that he had never been in a canoe in his life till he came to Mariposa, and that he sat four pews back in Dean Drone's church, and that his salary was eight hundred dollars. Beyond that, she didn't know a thing about him. She presumed, however, that the reason why he went past so fast was because he didn't dare to go slow.

This, of course, was perfectly correct. Ever since the day when Mr. Pupkin met Zena in the Main Street he used to come past the house on his bicycle just after bank hours. He would have gone past twenty times a day but he was afraid to. As he came up Oneida Street, he used to pedal faster and faster, – he never meant to, but he couldn't help it, – till he went past the piazza where Zena was sitting at an awful speed with his little yellow blazer flying in the wind. In a second he had disappeared in a buzz and a cloud of dust, and the momentum of it carried him clear out into the country for miles and miles before he ever dared to pause or look back.

Then Mr. Pupkin would ride in a huge circuit about the country, trying to think he was looking at the crops, and sooner or later his bicycle would be turned towards the town again and headed for Oneida Street, and would get going quicker and quicker and quicker, till the pedals whirled round with a buzz and he came past the judge's house again, like a bullet out of a gun. He rode fifteen miles to pass the house twice, and even then it took all the nerve that he had.

The people on Oneida Street thought that Mr. Pupkin was crazy, but Zena Pepperleigh knew that he was not. Already, you see, there was a sort of dim parallel between the passing of the bicycle and the last ride of Tancred the Inconsolable along the banks of the Danube.

I have already mentioned, I think, how Mr. Pupkin and Zena Pepperleigh first came to know one another. Like everything else about them, it was a sheer matter of coincidence, quite inexplicable unless you understand that these things are fore-ordained.

That, of course, is the way with fore-ordained affairs and that's where they differ from ordinary love.

I won't even try to describe how Mr. Pupkin felt when he first spoke with Zena and sat beside her as they copied out the "endless chain" letter asking for ten cents. They wrote out, as I said, no less than eight of the letters between them, and they found out that their handwritings were so alike that you could hardly tell them apart, except that Pupkin's letters were round and Zena's letters were pointed and Pupkin wrote straight up and down and Zena wrote on a slant. Beyond that the writing was so alike that it was the strangest coincidence in the world. Of course when they made figures it was different and Pupkin explained to Zena that in the bank you have to be able to make a seven so that it doesn't look like a nine.

So, as I say, they wrote the letters all afternoon and when it was over they walked up Oneida Street together, ever so slowly. When they got near the house, Zena asked

Pupkin to come in to tea, with such an easy off-hand way that you couldn't have told that she was half an hour late and was taking awful chances on the judge. Pupkin hadn't had time to say yes before the judge appeared at the door, just as they were stepping up on to the piazza, and he had a table napkin in his hand and the dynamite sparks were flying from his spectacles as he called out:

"Great heaven! Zena, why in everlasting blazes can't you get in to tea at a Christian hour?"

Zena gave one look of appeal to Pupkin, and Pupkin looked one glance of comprehension, and turned and fled down Oneida Street. And if the scene wasn't quite as dramatic as the renunciation of Tancred the Troubadour, it at least had something of the same elements in it.

Pupkin walked home to his supper at the Mariposa House on air, and that evening there was a gentle distance in his manner towards Sadie, the dining-room girl, that I suppose no bank clerk in Mariposa ever showed before. It was like Sir Galahad talking with the tire-women of Queen Guinevere and receiving huckleberry pie at their hands.

After that Mr. Pupkin and Zena Pepperleigh constantly met together. They played tennis as partners on the grass court behind Dr. Gallagher's house, – the Mariposa Tennis Club rent it, you remember, for fifty cents a month, – and Pupkin used to perform perfect prodigies of valour, leaping in the air to serve with his little body hooked like a letter S. Sometimes, too, they went out on Lake Wissanotti in the evening in Pupkin's canoe, with Zena sitting in the bow and Pupkin paddling in the stern and they went out ever so far and it was after dark and the stars were shining before they came home. Zena would look at the stars and say how infinitely far away they seemed, and Pupkin would realize that a girl with a mind like that couldn't have any use for a fool such as him. Zena used to ask him to point out the Pleiades and Jupiter and Ursa minor, and Pupkin showed her exactly where they were. That impressed them both tremendously, because Pupkin didn't know that Zena remembered the names out of the astronomy book at her boarding-school, and Zena didn't know that Pupkin simply took a chance on where the stars were.

And ever so many times they talked so intimately that Pupkin came mighty near telling her about his home in the Maritime Provinces and about his father and mother, and then kicked himself that he hadn't the manliness to speak straight out about it and take the consequences.

Please don't imagine from any of this that the course of Mr. Pupkin's love ran smooth. On the contrary, Pupkin himself felt that it was absolutely hopeless from the start.

There were, it might be admitted, certain things that seemed to indicate progress.

In the course of the months of June and July and August, he had taken Zena out in his canoe thirty-one times. Allowing an average of two miles for each evening, Pupkin had paddled Zena sixty-two miles, or more than a hundred thousand yards. That surely was something.

He had played tennis with her on sixteen afternoons. Three times he had left his tennis racket up at the judge's house in Zena's charge, and once he had, with her full consent, left his bicycle there all night. This must count for something. No girl could trifle with a man to the extent of having his bicycle leaning against the verandah post all night and mean nothing by it.

More than that – he had been to tea at the judge's house fourteen times, and seven times he had been asked by Lilian Drone to the rectory when Zena was coming, and five times by Nora Gallagher to tea at the doctor's house because Zena was there.

Altogether he had eaten so many meals where Zena was that his meal ticket at the Mariposa lasted nearly double its proper time, and the face of Sadie, the dining-room girl, had grown to wear a look of melancholy resignation, sadder than romance.

Still more than that, Pupkin had bought for Zena, reckoning it altogether, about two buckets of ice cream and perhaps half a bushel of chocolate. Not that Pupkin grudged the expense of it. On the contrary, over and above the ice cream and the chocolate he had bought her a white waistcoat and a walking stick with a gold top, a lot of new neckties and a pair of patent leather boots – that is, they were all bought on account of her, which is the same thing.

Add to all this that Pupkin and Zena had been to the Church of England Church nearly every Sunday evening for two months, and one evening they had even gone to the Presbyterian Church "for fun," which, if you know Mariposa, you will realize to be a wild sort of escapade that ought to speak volumes.

Yet in spite of this, Pupkin felt that the thing was hopeless: which only illustrates the dreadful ups and downs, the wild alternations of hope and despair that characterise an exceptional affair of this sort.

Yes, it was hopeless.

Every time that Pupkin watched Zena praying in church, he knew that she was too good for him. Every time that he came to call for her and found her reading Browning and Omar Khayyam he knew that she was too clever for him. And every time that he saw her at all he realized that she was too beautiful for him.

You see, Pupkin knew that he wasn't a hero. When Zena would clasp her hands and talk rapturously about crusaders and soldiers and firemen and heroes generally, Pupkin knew just where he came in. Not in it, that was all. If a war could have broken out in Mariposa, or the judge's house been invaded by the Germans, he might have had a chance, but as it was – hopeless.

Then there was Zena's father. Heaven knows Pupkin tried hard to please the judge. He agreed with every theory that Judge Pepperleigh advanced, and that took a pretty pliable intellect in itself. They denounced female suffrage one day and they favoured it the next. One day the judge would claim that the labour movement was eating out the heart of the country, and the next day he would hold that the hope of the world lay in the organization of the toiling masses. Pupkin shifted his opinions like the glass in a kaleidoscope. Indeed, the only things on which he was allowed to maintain a steadfast conviction were the purity of the Conservative Party of Canada and the awful wickedness of the recall of judges.

But with all that the judge was hardly civil to Pupkin. He hadn't asked him to the house till Zena brought him there, though, as a rule, all the bank clerks in Mariposa treated Judge Pepperleigh's premises as their own. He used to sit and sneer at Pupkin after he had gone till Zena would throw down the *Pioneers of Tecumseh Township* in a temper and flounce off the piazza to her room. After which the judge's manner would change instantly and he would relight his corn cob pipe and sit and positively beam with contentment. In all of which there was something so mysterious as to prove that Mr. Pupkin's chances were hopeless.

Nor was that all of it. Pupkin's salary was eight hundred dollars a year and the Exchange Bank limit for marriage was a thousand.

I suppose you are aware of the grinding capitalistic tyranny of the banks in Mariposa whereby marriage is put beyond the reach of ever so many mature and experienced men of nineteen and twenty and twenty-one, who are compelled to go on eating on a meal ticket at the Mariposa House and living over the bank to suit the whim of a group of capitalists.

Whenever Pupkin thought of this two hundred dollars he understood all that it meant by social unrest. In fact, he interpreted all forms of social discontent in terms of it. Russian Anarchism, German Socialism, the Labour Movement, Henry George, Lloyd George, – he understood the whole lot of them by thinking of his two hundred dollars.

When I tell you that at this period Mr. Pupkin read *Memoirs of the Great Revolutionists* and even thought of blowing up Henry Mullins with dynamite, you can appreciate his state of mind.

But not even by all these hindrances and obstacles to his love for Zena Pepperleigh would Peter Pupkin have been driven to commit suicide (oh, yes; he committed it three times, as I'm going to tell you), had it not been for another thing that he knew stood once and for all and in cold reality between him and Zena.

He felt it in a sort of way, as soon as he knew her. Each time that he tried to talk to her about his home and his father and mother and found that something held him back, he realized more and more the kind of thing that stood between them. Most of all did he realize it, with a sudden sickness of heart, when he got word that his father and mother wanted to come to Mariposa to see him and he had all he could do to head them off from it.

Why? Why stop them? The reason was, simple enough, that Pupkin was ashamed of them, bitterly ashamed. The picture of his mother and father turning up in Mariposa and being seen by his friends there and going up to the Pepperleigh's house made him feel faint with shame.

No, I don't say it wasn't wrong. It only shows what difference of fortune, the difference of being rich and being poor, means in this world. You perhaps have been so lucky that you cannot appreciate what it means to feel shame at the station of your own father and mother. You think it doesn't matter, that honesty and kindliness of heart are all that counts. That only shows that you have never known some of the bitterest feelings of people less fortunate than yourself.

So it was with Mr. Pupkin. When he thought of his father and mother turning up in Mariposa, his face reddened with unworthy shame.

He could just picture the scene! He could see them getting out of their Limousine touring car, with the chauffeur holding open the door for them, and his father asking for a suite of rooms, – just think of it, a suite of rooms! – at the Mariposa House.

The very thought of it turned him ill.

What! You have mistaken my meaning? Ashamed of them because they were poor? Good heavens, no, but because they were rich! And not rich in the sense in which they use the term in Mariposa, where a rich person merely means a man who has money enough to build a house with a piazza and to have everything he wants; but rich in the other sense, – motor cars, Ritz hotels, steam yachts, summer islands and all that sort of thing.

Why, Pupkin's father, – what's the use of trying to conceal it any longer? – was the senior partner in the law firm of Pupkin, Pupkin, and Pupkin. If you know the Maritime Provinces at all, you've heard of the Pupkins. The name is a household word from Chedabucto to Chidabecto. And, for the matter of that, the law firm and the fact that Pupkin senior had been an Attorney General was the least part of it. Attorney General! Why, there's no money in that! It's no better than the Senate. No, no, Pupkin senior, like so many lawyers, was practically a promoter, and he blew companies like bubbles, and when he wasn't in the Maritime Provinces he was in Boston and New York raising money and floating loans, and when they had no money left in New York he floated it in London: and when he had it, he floated on top of it big rafts of lumber on the Miramichi and codfish on the Grand Banks and lesser fish in the Fundy Bay. You've heard perhaps of the Tidal Transportation Company, and Fundy Fisheries Corporation, and the Paspebiac Pulp and Paper Unlimited?

The PUPKINS

Well, all of those were Pupkin senior under other names. So just imagine him in Mariposa! Wouldn't he be utterly foolish there? Just imagine him meeting Jim Eliot and treating him like a druggist merely because he ran a drug store! or speaking to Jefferson Thorpe as if he were a barber simply because he shaved for money! Why, a man like that could ruin young Pupkin in Mariposa in half a day, and Pupkin knew it.

That wouldn't matter so much, but think of the Pepperleighs and Zena! Everything would be over with them at once. Pupkin knew just what the judge thought of riches and luxuries. How often had he heard the judge pass sentences of life imprisonment on Pierpont Morgan and Mr. Rockefeller. How often had Pupkin heard him say that any man who received more than three thousand dollars a year (that was the judicial salary in the Missinaba district) was a mere robber, unfit to shake the hand of an honest man. Bitter! I should think he was! He was not so bitter, perhaps, as Mr. Muddleson, the principal of the Mariposa high school, who said that any man who received more than fifteen hundred dollars was a public enemy. He was certainly not so bitter as Trelawney, the post-master, who said that any man who got from society more than thirteen hundred dollars (apart from a legitimate increase in recognition of a successful election) was a danger to society. Still, he was bitter. They all were in Mariposa. Pupkin could just imagine how they would despise his father!

And Zena! That was the worst of all. How often had Pupkin heard her say that she simply hated diamonds, wouldn't wear them, despised them, wouldn't give a thank you for a whole tiara of them! As for motor cars and steam yachts, – well, it was pretty plain that that sort of thing had no chance with Zena Pepperleigh. Why, she had told Pupkin one night in the canoe that she would only marry a man who was poor and had his way to make and would hew down difficulties for her sake. And when Pupkin couldn't answer the argument she was quite cross and silent all the way home.

What was Peter Pupkin doing, then, at eight hundred dollars in a bank in Mariposa? If you ask that, it means that you know nothing of the life of the Maritime Provinces and the sturdy temper of the people. I suppose there are no people in the world who hate luxury and extravagance and that sort of thing quite as much as the Maritime Province people, and, of them, no one hated luxury more than Pupkin senior.

Don't mistake the man. He wore a long sealskin coat in winter, yes; but mark you, not as a matter of luxury, but merely as a question of his lungs. He smoked, I admit it, a thirty-five cent cigar, not because he preferred it, but merely through a delicacy of the thorax that made it imperative. He drank champagne at lunch, I concede the point, not in the least from the enjoyment of it, but simply on account of a peculiar affection of the tongue and lips that positively dictated it. His own longing – and his wife shared it – was for the simple, simple life – an island somewhere, with birds and trees. They had bought three or four islands – one in the St. Lawrence, and two in the Gulf, and one off the coast of Maine – looking for this sort of thing. Pupkin senior often said that he wanted to have some place that would remind him of the little old farm up the Aroostook where he was brought up. He often bought little old farms, just to try them, but they always turned out to be so near a city that he cut them into real estate lots, without even having had time to look at them.

But – and this is where the emphasis lay – in the matter of luxury for his only son, Peter, Pupkin senior was a Maritime Province man right to the core, with all the hardihood of the United Empire Loyalists ingrained in him. No luxury for that boy! No, sir! From his childhood, Pupkin senior had undertaken, at the least sign of luxury, to "tan it out of him," after the fashion still in vogue in the provinces. Then he sent him to an old-fashioned school to get it "thumped out of him," and after that he had put him for a year on a Nova Scotia schooner to get it "knocked out of him." If, after all that, young Pupkin, even when he came to Mariposa, wore cameo pins and daffodil blazers, and broke out into ribbed silk saffron ties on pay day, it only shows that the old Adam still needs further tanning even in the Maritime Provinces.

Young Pupkin, of course, was to have gone into law. That was his father's cherished dream and would have made the firm Pupkin, Pupkin, Pupkin, and Pupkin, as it ought to have been. But young Peter was kept out of the law by the fool system of examinations devised since his father's time. Hence there was nothing for it but to sling him into a bank; "sling him" was, I think, the expression. So his father decided that if Pupkin was to be slung, he should be slung good and far – clean into Canada (you know the way they use that word in the Maritime Provinces). And to sling Pupkin he called in the services of an old friend, a man after his own heart, just as violent as himself, who used to be at the law school in the city with Pupkin senior thirty years ago. So this friend, who happened to live in Mariposa, and who was a violent man, said at once: "Edward, by Jehoshaphat! send the boy up here."

So that is how Pupkin came to Mariposa. And if, when he got there, his father's friend gave no sign, and treated the boy with roughness and incivility, that may have been, for all I know, a continuation of the "tanning" process of the Maritime people.

Did I mention that the Pepperleigh family, generations ago, had taken up land near the Aroostook, and that it was from there the judge's father came to Tecumseh Township? Perhaps not, but it doesn't matter.

But surely after such reminiscences as these the awful things that are impending over Mr. Pupkin must be kept for another chapter.

BANK
DETECTIVES

# THE **MARIPOSA**
# **BANK MYSTERY**

**S**UICIDE IS A THING that ought not to be committed without very careful thought. It often involves serious consequences, and in some cases brings pain to others than oneself.

I don't say that there is no justification for it. There often is. Anybody who has listened to certain kinds of music, or read certain kinds of poetry, or heard certain kinds of performances upon the concertina, will admit that there are some lives which ought not to be continued, and that even suicide has its brighter aspects.

But to commit suicide on grounds of love is at the best a very dubious experiment. I know that in this I am expressing an opinion contrary to that of most true lovers who embrace suicide on the slightest provocation as the only honourable termination of an existence that never ought to have begun.

I quite admit that there is a glamour and a sensation about the thing which has its charm, and that there is nothing like it for causing a girl to realize the value of the heart that she has broken and which breathed forgiveness upon her at the very moment when it held in its hand the half-pint of prussic acid that was to terminate its beating for ever.

But apart from the general merits of the question, I suppose there are few people, outside of lovers, who know what it is to commit suicide four times in five weeks.

Yet this was what happened to Mr. Pupkin, of the Exchange Bank of Mariposa.

Ever since he had known Zena Pepperleigh he had realized that his love for her was hopeless. She was too beautiful for him and too good for him; her father hated him and her mother despised him; his salary was too small and his own people were too rich.

If you add to all that that he came up to the judge's house one night and found a poet reciting verses to Zena, you will understand the suicide at once. It was one of those regular poets with a solemn jackass face, and lank parted hair and eyes like puddles of molasses. I don't know how he came there – up from the city, probably – but there he was on the Pepperleighs' verandah that August evening. He was reciting poetry – either Tennyson's or Shelley's, or his own, you couldn't tell – and about him sat Zena with her hands clasped and Nora Gallagher looking at the sky and Jocelyn Drone gazing into infinity, and a little tubby woman looking at the poet with her head falling over sideways – in fact, there was a whole group of them.

I don't know what it is about poets that draws women to them in this way. But everybody knows that a poet has only to sit and saw the air with his hands and recite verses in a deep stupid voice, and all the women are crazy over him. Men despise him and would kick him off the verandah if they dared, but the women simply rave over him.

So Pupkin sat there in the gloom and listened to this poet reciting Browning and he realized that everybody understood it but him. He could see Zena with her eyes fixed on the poet as if she were hanging on to every syllable (she was; she needed to), and he stood it just about fifteen minutes and then slid off the side of the verandah and disappeared without even saying good-night.

He walked straight down Oneida Street and along the Main Street just as hard as he could go. There was only one purpose in his mind, – suicide. He was heading straight for Jim Eliot's drug store on the main corner and his idea was to buy a drink of chloroform and drink it and die right there on the spot.

As Pupkin walked down the street, the whole thing was so vivid in his mind that he could picture it to the remotest detail. He could even see it all in type, in big headings in the newspapers of the following day:

APPALLING SUICIDE.

PETER PUPKIN POISONED.

He perhaps hoped that the thing might lead to some kind of public enquiry and that the question of Browning's poetry and whether it is altogether fair to allow of its general circulation would be fully ventilated in the newspapers.

Thinking of that, Pupkin came to the main corner.

On a warm August evening the drug store of Mariposa, as you know, is all a blaze of lights. You can hear the hissing of the soda-water fountain half a block away, and inside the store there are ever so many people – boys and girls and old people too – all drinking sarsaparilla and chocolate sundaes and lemon sours and foaming drinks that you take out of long straws. There is such a laughing and a talking as you never heard, and the girls are all in white and pink and cambridge blue, and the soda fountain is of white marble with silver taps, and it hisses and sputters, and Jim Eliot and his assistant wear white coats with red geraniums in them, and it's just as gay as gay.

The foyer of the opera in Paris may be a fine sight, but I doubt if it can compare with the inside of Eliot's drug store in Mariposa – for real gaiety and joy of living.

This night the store was especially crowded because it was a Saturday and that meant early closing for all the hotels, except, of course, Smith's. So as the hotels were shut, the people were all in the drug store, drinking like fishes. It just shows the folly of Local Option and the Temperance Movement and all that. Why, if you shut the hotels you simply drive the people to the soda fountains and there's more drinking than ever, and not only of the men, too, but the girls and young boys and children. I've seen little things of eight and nine that had to be lifted up on the high stools at Eliot's drug store, drinking great goblets of lemon soda, enough to burst them – brought there by their own fathers, and why? Simply because the hotel bars were shut.

What's the use of thinking you can stop people drinking merely by cutting off whiskey and brandy? The only effect is to drive them to taking lemon sour and sarsaparilla and cherry pectoral and caroka cordial and things they wouldn't have touched before. So in the long run they drink more than ever. The point is that you can't prevent people having a good time, no matter how hard you try. If they can't have it with lager beer and brandy, they'll have it with plain soda and lemon pop, and so the whole gloomy scheme of the temperance people breaks down, anyway.

But I was only saying that Eliot's drug store in Mariposa on a Saturday night is the gayest and brightest spot in the world.

And just imagine what a fool of a place to commit suicide in!

Just imagine going up to the soda-water fountain and asking for five cents' worth of chloroform and soda! Well, you simply can't, that's all.

That's the way Pupkin found it. You see, as soon as he came in, somebody called out: "Hello, Pete!" and one or two others called: "Hullo, Pup!" and some said: "How goes it?" and others: "How are you toughing it?" and so on, because you see they had all been drinking more or less and naturally they felt jolly and glad-hearted.

So the upshot of it was that instead of taking chloroform, Pupkin stepped up to the counter of the fountain and he had a bromo-seltzer with cherry soda, and after that he had one of those aerated seltzers, and then a couple of lemon seltzers and a bromophizzer.

I don't know if you know the mental effect of a bromo-seltzer.

SONS of TEMPERANCE

But it's a hard thing to commit suicide on.

You can't.

You feel so buoyant.

Anyway, what with the phizzing of the seltzer and the lights and the girls, Pupkin began to feel so fine that he didn't care a cuss for all the Browning in the world, and as for the poet – oh, to blazes with him! What's poetry, anyway? – only rhymes.

So, would you believe it, in about ten minutes Peter Pupkin was off again and heading straight for the Pepperleighs' house, poet or no poet, and, what was more to the point, he carried with him three great bricks of Eliot's ice cream – in green, pink and brown layers. He struck the verandah just at the moment when Browning was getting too stale and dreary for words. His brain was all sizzling and jolly with the bromo-seltzer, and when he fetched out the ice cream bricks and Zena ran to get plates and spoons to eat it with, and Pupkin went with her to help fetch them and they picked out the spoons together, they were so laughing and happy that it was just a marvel. Girls, you know, need no bromo-seltzer. They're full of it all the time.

And as for the poet – well, can you imagine how Pupkin felt when Zena told him that the poet was married, and that the tubby little woman with her head on sideways was his wife?

So they had the ice cream, and the poet ate it in bucketsful. Poets always do. They need it. And after it the poet recited some stanzas of his own and Pupkin saw that he had misjudged the man, because it was dandy poetry, the very best. That night Pupkin walked home on air and there was no thought of chloroform, and it turned out that he hadn't committed suicide, but like all lovers he had commuted it.

I don't need to describe in full the later suicides of Mr. Pupkin, because they were all conducted on the same plan and rested on something the same reasons as above.

Sometimes he would go down at night to the offices of the bank below his bedroom and bring up his bank revolver in order to make an end of himself with it. This, too, he could see headed up in the newspapers as:

BRILLIANT BOY BANKER

BLOWS OUT BRAINS.

But blowing your brains out is a noisy, rackety performance, and Pupkin soon found that only special kinds of brains are suited for it. So he always sneaked back again later in the night and put the revolver in its place, deciding to drown himself instead. Yet every time that he walked down to the Trestle Bridge over the Ossawippi he found it was quite unsuitable for drowning – too high, and the water too swift and black, and the rushes too gruesome – in fact, not at all the kind of place for a drowning.

Far better, he realized, to wait there on the railroad track and throw himself under the wheels of the express and be done with it. Yet, though Pupkin often waited in this way for the train, he was never able to pick out a pair of wheels that suited him. Anyhow, it's awfully hard to tell an express from a fast freight.

I wouldn't mention these attempts at suicide if one of them hadn't finally culminated in making Peter Pupkin a

hero and solving for him the whole perplexed entangle-
ment of his love affair with Zena Pepperleigh. Incidentally
it threw him into the very centre of one of the most impenetrable bank mysteries that ever baffled the ingenuity of
some of the finest legal talent that ever adorned one of the
most enterprising communities in the country.

It happened one night, as I say, that Pupkin decided
to go down into the office of the bank and get his revolver
and see if it would blow his brains out. It was the night
of the Firemen's Ball and Zena had danced four times
with a visitor from the city, a man who was in the fourth
year at the University and who knew everything. It was
more than Peter Pupkin could bear. Mallory Tompkins
was away that night, and when Pupkin came home he was
all alone in the building, except for Gillis, the caretaker,
who lived in the extension at the back.

He sat in his room for hours brooding. Two or three
times he picked up a book – he remembered afterwards
distinctly that it was *Kant's Critique of Pure Reason* – and
tried to read it, but it seemed meaningless and trivial. Then
with a sudden access of resolution he started from his chair
and made his way down the stairs and into the office room
of the bank, meaning to get a revolver and kill himself on
the spot and let them find his body lying on the floor.

It was then far on in the night and the empty building
of the bank was as still as death. Pupkin could hear the
stairs creak under his feet, and as he went he thought he
heard another sound like the opening or closing of a door.
But it sounded not like the sharp ordinary noise of a closing
door but with a dull muffled noise as if someone had shut
the iron door of a safe in a room under the ground. For a

moment Pupkin stood and listened with his heart thumping against his ribs. Then he kicked his slippers from his feet and without a sound stole into the office on the ground floor and took the revolver from his teller's desk. As he gripped it, he listened to the sounds on the back-stairway and in the vaults below.

I should explain that in the Exchange Bank of Mariposa the offices are on the ground floor level with the street. Below this is another floor with low dark rooms paved with flagstones, with unused office desks and with piles of papers stored in boxes. On this floor are the vaults of the bank, and lying in them in the autumn – the grain season – there is anything from fifty to a hundred thou sand dollars in currency tied in bundles. There is no other light down there than the dim reflection from the lights out on the street, that lies in patches on the stone floor.

I think as Peter Pupkin stood, revolver in hand, in the office of the bank, he had forgotten all about the maudlin purpose of his first coming. He had forgotten for the moment all about heroes and love affairs, and his whole mind was focussed, sharp and alert, with the intensity of the night-time, on the sounds that he heard in the vault and on the back-stairway of the bank.

Straight away Pupkin knew what it meant as plainly as if it were written in print. He had forgotten, I say, about being a hero and he only knew that there was sixty thou-sand dollars in the vault of the bank below, and that he was paid eight hundred dollars a year to look after it.

As Peter Pupkin stood there listening to the sounds in his stockinged feet, his face showed grey as ashes in the light that fell through the window from the street. His heart beat like a hammer against his ribs. But behind its beatings was the blood of four generations of Loyalists, and the robber who would take that sixty thousand dollars from the Mariposa bank must take it over the dead body of Peter Pupkin, teller.

Pupkin walked down the stairs to the lower room, the one below the ground with the bank vault in it, with as fine a step as any of his ancestors showed on parade. And if he had known it, as he came down the stairway in the front of the vault room, there was a man crouched in the shadow of the passage way by the stairs at the back. This man, too, held a revolver in his hand, and, criminal or not, his face was as resolute as Pupkin's own. As he heard the teller's step on the stair, he turned and waited in the shadow of the doorway without a sound.

There is no need really to mention all these details. They are only of interest as showing how sometimes a bank teller in a corded smoking jacket and stockinged feet may be turned into such a hero as even the Mariposa girls might dream about.

All of this must have happened at about three o'clock in the night. This much was established afterwards from the evidence of Gillis, the caretaker. When he first heard the sounds he had looked at his watch and noticed that it was half-past two; the watch he knew was three-quarters of an hour slow three days before and had been gaining since. The exact time at which Gillis heard footsteps in the bank and started downstairs, pistol in hand, became a nice point afterwards in the cross-examination.

But one must not anticipate. Pupkin reached the iron

door of the bank safe, and knelt in front of it, feeling in the dark to find the fracture of the lock. As he knelt, he heard a sound behind him, and swung round on his knees and saw the bank robber in the half light of the passage way and the glitter of a pistol in his hand. The rest was over in an instant. Pupkin heard a voice that was his own, but that sounded strange and hollow, call out: "Drop that, or I'll fire!" and then just as he raised his revolver, there came a blinding flash of light before his eyes, and Peter Pupkin, junior teller of the bank, fell forward on the floor and knew no more.

At that point, of course, I ought to close down a chapter, or volume, or, at least, strike the reader over the head with a sandbag to force him to stop and think. In common fairness one ought to stop here and count a hundred or get up and walk round a block, or, at any rate, picture to oneself Peter Pupkin lying on the floor of the bank, motionless, his arms distended, the revolver still grasped in his hand. But I must go on.

By half-past seven on the following morning it was known all over Mariposa that Peter Pupkin the junior teller of the Exchange had been shot dead by a bank robber in the vault of the building. It was known also that Gillis, the caretaker, had been shot and killed at the foot of the stairs, and that the robber had made off with fifty thousand dollars in currency; that he had left a trail of blood on the sidewalk and that the men were out tracking him with bloodhounds in the great swamps to the north of the town.

This, I say, and it is important to note it, was what they knew at half-past seven. Of course as each hour went past they learned more and more. At eight o'clock it was known that Pupkin was not dead, but dangerously wounded in the lungs. At eight-thirty it was known that he was not shot in the lungs, but that the ball had traversed the pit of his stomach.

At nine o'clock it was learned that the pit of Pupkin's stomach was all right, but that the bullet had struck his right ear and carried it away. Finally it was learned that his ear had not exactly been carried away, that is, not precisely removed by the bullet, but that it had grazed Pupkin's head in such a way that it had stunned him, and if it had been an inch or two more to the left it might have reached his brain. This, of course, was just as good as being killed from the point of view of public interest.

Indeed, by nine o'clock Pupkin could be himself seen on the Main Street with a great bandage sideways on his head, pointing out the traces of the robber. Gillis, the caretaker, too, it was known by eight, had not been killed. He had been shot through the brain, but whether the injury was serious or not was only a matter of conjecture. In fact, by ten o'clock it was understood that the bullet from the robber's second shot had grazed the side of the caretaker's head, but as far as could be known his brain was just as before. I should add that the first report about the bloodstains and the swamp and the bloodhounds turned out to be inaccurate. The stains may have been blood, but as they led to the cellar way of Netley's store they may have also been molasses, though it was argued, to be sure, that the robber might well have poured molasses over the bloodstains from sheer cunning.

It was remembered, too, that there were no bloodhounds in Mariposa, although, mind you, there are any amount of dogs there.

So you see that by ten o'clock in the morning the whole affair was settling into the impenetrable mystery which it ever since remained.

Not that there wasn't evidence enough. There was Pupkin's own story and Gillis's story, and the stories of all the people who had heard the shots and seen the robber (some said, the bunch of robbers) go running past (others said, walking past), in the night. Apparently the robber ran up and down half the streets of Mariposa before he vanished.

But the stories of Pupkin and Gillis were plain enough. Pupkin related that he heard sounds in the bank and came downstairs just in time to see the robber crouching in the passage way, and that the robber was a large, hulking, villainous looking man, wearing a heavy coat. Gillis told exactly the same story, having heard the noises at the same time, except that he first described the robber as a small thin fellow (peculiarly villainous looking, however, even in the dark), wearing a short jacket; but on thinking it over, Gillis realized that he had been wrong about the size of the criminal, and that he was even bigger, if anything, than what Mr. Pupkin thought. Gillis had fired at the robber; just at the same moment had Mr. Pupkin.

Beyond that, all was mystery, absolute and impenetrable.

By eleven o'clock the detectives had come up from the city under orders from the head of the bank.

I wish you could have seen the two detectives as they moved to and fro in Mariposa – fine looking, stern, impenetrable men that they were. They seemed to take in the whole town by instinct and so quietly. They found their way to Mr. Smith's Hotel just as quietly as if it wasn't design at all and stood there at the bar, picking up scraps of conversation – you know the way detectives do it. Occasionally they allowed one or two bystanders – confederates, perhaps, – to buy a drink for them, and you could see from the way they drank it that they were still listening for a clue. If there had been the faintest clue in Smith's Hotel or in the Mariposa House or in the Continental, those fellows would have been at it like a flash.

To see them moving round the town that day – silent, massive, imperturbable – gave one a great idea of their strange, dangerous calling. They went about the town all day and yet in such a quiet peculiar way that you couldn't have realized that they were working at all. They ate their dinner together at Smith's café and took an hour and a half over it to throw people off the scent. Then when they got them off it, they sat and talked with Josh Smith in the back bar to keep them off. Mr. Smith seemed to take to them right away. They were men of his own size, or near it, and anyway hotel men and detectives have a general affinity and share in the same impenetrable silence and in their confidential knowledge of the weaknesses of the public.

Mr. Smith, too, was of great use to the detectives. "Boys," he said, "I wouldn't ask too close as to what folks was out late at night: in this town it don't do."

When those two great brains finally left for the city on the five-thirty, it was hard to realize that behind each grand, impassible face a perfect vortex of clues was seething.

But if the detectives were heroes, what was Pupkin? Imagine him with his bandage on his head standing in front of the bank and talking of the midnight robbery with that peculiar false modesty that only heroes are entitled to use.

I don't know whether you have ever been a hero, but for sheer exhilaration there is nothing like it. And for Mr. Pupkin, who had gone through life thinking himself no good, to be suddenly exalted into the class of Napoleon Bonaparte and John Maynard and the Charge of the Light Brigade – oh, it was wonderful. Because Pupkin was a brave man now and he knew it and acquired with it all the brave man's modesty. In fact, I believe he was heard to say that he had only done his duty, and that what he did was what any other man would have done, though when somebody else said: "That's so, when you come to think of it," Pupkin turned on him that quiet look of the wounded hero, bitterer than words.

And if Pupkin had known that all of the afternoon papers in the city reported him dead, he would have felt more luxurious still.

That afternoon the Mariposa court sat in enquiry, – technically it was summoned in inquest on the dead robber – though they hadn't found the body – and it was wonderful to see them lining up the witnesses and holding cross-examinations. There is something in the cross-examination of great criminal lawyers like Nivens, of Mariposa, and in the counter examinations of presiding judges like Pepperleigh that thrills you to the core with the astuteness of it.

They had Henry Mullins, the manager, on the stand for an hour and a half, and the excitement was so breathless that you could have heard a pin drop. Nivens took him on first.

"What is your name?" he said.

"Henry August Mullins."

"What position do you hold?"

"I am manager of the Exchange Bank."

"When were you born?"

"December 30, 1869."

After that, Nivens stood looking quietly at Mullins. You could feel that he was thinking pretty deeply before he shot the next question at him.

"Where did you go to school?"

Mullins answered straight off: "The high school down home," and Nivens thought again for a while and then asked:

"How many boys were at the school?"

"About sixty."

"How many masters?"

"About three."

After that Nivens paused a long while and seemed to be digesting the evidence, but at last an idea seemed to strike him and he said:

"I understand you were not on the bank premises last night. Where were you?"

"Down the lake duck shooting."

You should have seen the excitement in the court when Mullins said this. The judge leaned forward in his chair and broke in at once.

"Did you get any, Harry?" he asked.

"Yes," Mullins said, "about six."

"Where did you get them? What? In the wild rice

marsh past the river? You don't say so! Did you get them on the sit or how?"

All of these questions were fired off at the witness from the court in a single breath. In fact, it was the knowledge that the first ducks of the season had been seen in the Ossawippi marsh that led to the termination of the proceedings before the afternoon was a quarter over. Mullins and George Duff and half the witnesses were off with shotguns as soon as the court was cleared.

I may as well state at once that the full story of the robbery of the bank of Mariposa never came to the light. A number of arrests – mostly of vagrants and suspicious characters – were made, but the guilt of the robbery was never brought home to them. One man was arrested twenty miles away, at the other end of Missinaba county, who not only corresponded exactly with the description of the robber, but, in addition to this, had a wooden leg. Vagrants with one leg are always regarded with suspicion in places like Mariposa, and whenever a robbery or a murder happens they are arrested in batches.

It was never known just how much money was stolen from the bank. Some people said ten thousand dollars, others more. The bank, no doubt for business motives, claimed that the contents of the safe were intact and that the robber had been foiled in his design.

But none of this matters to the exaltation of Mr. Pupkin. Good fortune, like bad, never comes in small instalments. On that wonderful day, every good thing happened to Peter Pupkin at once. The morning saw him a hero. At the sitting of the court, the judge publicly told him that his conduct was fit to rank among the annals of the pioneers of Tecumseh Township, and asked him to his house for supper. At five o'clock he received the telegram of promotion from the head office that raised his salary to a thousand dollars, and made him not only a hero but a marriageable man. At six o'clock he started up to the judge's house with his resolution nerved to the most momentous step of his life.

His mind was made up.

He would do a thing seldom if ever done in Mariposa. He would propose to Zena Pepperleigh. In Mariposa this kind of step, I say, is seldom taken. The course of love runs on and on through all its stages of tennis playing and dancing and sleigh riding, till by sheer notoriety of circumstance an understanding is reached. To propose straight out would be thought priggish and affected and is supposed to belong only to people in books.

But Pupkin felt that what ordinary people dare not do, heroes are allowed to attempt. He would propose to Zena, and more than that, he would tell her in a straight, manly way that he was rich and take the consequences.

And he did it.

That night on the piazza, where the hammock hangs in the shadow of the Virginia creeper, he did it. By sheer good luck the judge had gone indoors to the library, and by a piece of rare good fortune Mrs. Pepperleigh had gone indoors to the sewing room, and by a happy trick of coincidence the servant was out and the dog was tied up – in fact, no such chain of circumstances was ever offered in favour of mortal man before.

The
VAGRANT

What Zena said – beyond saying yes – I do not know. I am sure that when Pupkin told her of the money, she bore up as bravely as so fine a girl as Zena would, and when he spoke of diamonds she said she would wear them for his sake.

They were saying these things and other things – ever so many other things – when there was such a roar and a clatter up Oneida Street as you never heard, and there came bounding up to the house one of the most marvellous Limousine touring cars that ever drew up at the home of a judge on a modest salary of three thousand dollars. When it stopped there sprang from it an excited man in a long sealskin coat – worn not for the luxury of it at all but from the sheer chilliness of the autumn evening. And it was, as of course you know, Pupkin's father. He had seen the news of his son's death in the evening paper in the city. They drove the car through, so the chauffeur said, in two hours and a quarter, and behind them there was to follow a special trainload of detectives and emergency men, but Pupkin senior had cancelled all that by telegram half way up when he heard that Peter was still living.

For a moment as his eye rested on young Pupkin you would almost have imagined, had you not known that he came from the Maritime Provinces, that there were tears in them and that he was about to hug his son to his heart. But if he didn't hug Peter to his heart, he certainly did within a few moments clasp Zena to it, in that fine fatherly way in which they clasp pretty girls in the Maritime Provinces. The strangest thing is that Pupkin senior seemed to understand the whole situation without any explanations at all.

Judge Pepperleigh, I think, would have shaken both of Pupkin senior's arms off when he saw him; and when you heard them call one another "Ned" and "Phillip" it made you feel that they were boys again attending classes together at the old law school in the city.

If Pupkin thought that his father wouldn't make a hit in Mariposa, it only showed his ignorance. Pupkin senior sat there on the judge's verandah smoking a corn cob pipe as if he had never heard of Havana cigars in his life. In the three days that he spent in Mariposa that autumn, he went in and out of Jeff Thorpe's barber shop and Eliot's drug store, shot black ducks in the marsh and played poker every evening at a hundred matches for a cent as if he had never lived any other life in all his days. They had to send him telegrams enough to fill a satchel to make him come away.

So Pupkin and Zena in due course of time were married, and went to live in one of the enchanted houses on the hillside in the newer part of the town, where you may find them to this day.

You may see Pupkin there at any time cutting enchanted grass on a little lawn in as gaudy a blazer as ever.

But if you step up to speak to him or walk with him into the enchanted house, pray modulate your voice a little – musical though it is – for there is said to be an enchanted baby on the premises whose sleep must not lightly be disturbed.

JOHN HENRY
BAGSHAW

# THE
# GREAT ELECTION IN MISSINABA COUNTY

**D**ON'T ASK ME what election it was, whether Dominion or Provincial or Imperial or Universal, for I scarcely know.

It must, of course, have been going on in other parts of the country as well, but I saw it all from Missinaba County which, with the town of Mariposa, was, of course, the storm centre and focus point of the whole turmoil.

I only know that it was a huge election and that on it turned issues of the most tremendous importance, such as whether or not Mariposa should become part of the United States, and whether the flag that had waved over the school house at Tecumseh Township for ten centuries should be trampled under the hoof of an alien invader, and whether Britons should be slaves, and whether Canadians should be Britons, and whether the farming class would prove themselves Canadians, and tremendous questions of that kind.

And there was such a roar and a tumult to it, and such a waving of flags and beating of drums and flaring of torchlights that such parts of the election as may have been going on elsewhere than in Missinaba county must have been quite unimportant and didn't really matter.

Now that it is all over, we can look back at it without heat or passion. We can see, – it's plain enough now, – that in the great election Canada saved the British Empire, and that Missinaba saved Canada and that the vote of the Third Concession of Tecumseh Township saved Missinaba County, and that those of us who carried the third concession, – well, there's no need to push it further. We prefer to be modest about it. If we still speak of it, it is only quietly and simply and not more than three or four times a day.

But you can't understand the election at all, and the conventions and the campaigns and the nominations and the balloting, unless you first appreciate the peculiar complexion of politics in Mariposa.

Let me begin at the beginning. Everybody in Mariposa is either a Liberal or a Conservative or else is both. Some of the people are or have been Liberals or Conservatives all their lives and are called dyed-in-the-wool Grits or old-time Tories and things of that sort. These people get from long training such a swift penetrating insight into national issues that they can decide the most complicated question in four seconds: in fact, just as soon as they grab the city papers out of the morning mail, they know the whole solution of any problem you can put to them. There are other people whose aim it is to be broad-minded and judicious and who vote Liberal or Conservative according to their judgment of the questions of the day. If their judgment of these questions tells them that there is something in it for them in voting Liberal, then they do so. But if not, they refuse to be the slaves of a party or the henchmen of any political leader. So that anybody looking for henches has got to keep away from them.

But the one thing that nobody is allowed to do in Mariposa is to have no politics. Of course there are always some people whose circumstances compel them to say that they have no politics. But that is easily understood. Take the case of Trelawney, the post-master. Long ago he was a letter carrier under the old Mackenzie Government, and later he was a letter sorter under the old Macdonald Government, and after that a letter stamper under the old Tupper Government, and so on. Trelawney always says that he has no politics, but the truth is that he has too many.

So, too, with the clergy in Mariposa. They have no politics – absolutely none. Yet Dean Drone round election time always announces as his text such a verse as: "Lo! is there not one righteous man in Israel?" or: "What ho! is it not time for a change?" And that is a signal for all the Liberal business men to get up and leave their pews.

Similarly over at the Presbyterian Church, the minister says that his sacred calling will not allow him to take part in politics and that his sacred calling prevents him from breathing even a word of harshness against his fellow man, but that when it comes to the elevation of the ungodly into high places in the commonwealth (this means, of course, the nomination of the Conservative candidate) then he's not going to allow his sacred calling to prevent him from saying just what he thinks of it. And by that time, having pretty well cleared the church of Conservatives, he proceeds to show from the scriptures that the ancient

Hebrews were Liberals to a man, except those who were drowned in the flood or who perished, more or less deservedly, in the desert.

There are, I say, some people who are allowed to claim to have no politics, – the office holders, and the clergy and the school teachers and the hotel keepers. But beyond them, anybody in Mariposa who says that he has no politics is looked upon as crooked, and people wonder what it is that he is "out after."

In fact, the whole town and county is a hive of politics, and people who have only witnessed gatherings such as the House of Commons at Westminster and the Senate at Washington and never seen a Conservative Convention at Tecumseh Corners or a Liberal Rally at the Concession school house, don't know what politics means.

So you may imagine the excitement in Mariposa when it became known that King George had dissolved the parliament of Canada and had sent out a writ or command for Missinaba County to elect for him some other person than John Henry Bagshaw because he no longer had confidence in him.

The king, of course, is very well known, very favourably known, in Mariposa. Everybody remembers how he visited the town on his great tour in Canada, and stopped off at the Mariposa station. Although he was only a prince at the time, there was quite a big crowd down at the depôt and everybody felt what a shame it was that the prince had no time to see more of Mariposa, because he would get such a false idea of it, seeing only the station and the lumber yards. Still, they all came to the station and all the Liberals and Conservatives mixed together perfectly freely and stood side by side without any distinction, so that the prince should not observe any party differences among them. And he didn't, – you could see that he didn't. They read him an address all about the tranquillity and loyalty of the Empire, and they purposely left out any reference to the trouble over the town wharf or the big row there had been about the location of the new post-office. There was a general decent feeling that it wouldn't be fair to disturb the prince with these things: later on, as king, he would, of course, *have* to know all about them, but meanwhile it was better to leave him with the idea that his empire was tranquil.

So they deliberately couched the address in terms that were just as reassuring as possible and the prince was simply delighted with it. I am certain that he slept pretty soundly after hearing that address. Why, you could see it taking effect even on his aides-de-camp and the people round him, so imagine how the prince must have felt!

I think in Mariposa they understand kings perfectly. Every time that a king or a prince comes, they try to make him see the bright side of everything and let him think that they're all united. Judge Pepperleigh walked up and down arm in arm with Dr. Gallagher, the worst Grit in the town, just to make the prince feel fine.

So when they got the news that the king had lost confidence in John Henry Bagshaw, the sitting member, they never questioned it a bit. Lost confidence? All right, they'd elect him another right away. They'd elect him half a dozen if he needed them. They don't mind; they'd elect the whole town man after man rather than have the king worried about it.

In any case, all the Conservatives had been wondering for years how the king and the governor-general and men like that had tolerated such a man as Bagshaw so long.

Missinaba County, I say, is a regular hive of politics, and not the miserable, crooked, money-ridden politics of the cities, but the straight, real old-fashioned thing that is an honour to the country side. Any man who would offer to take a bribe or sell his convictions for money would be an object of scorn. I don't say they wouldn't take money, – they would, of course, why not? – but if they did they would take it in a straight fearless way and say nothing about it. They might, – it's only human, – accept a job or a contract from the government, but if they did, rest assured it would be in a broad national spirit and not for the sake of the work itself. No, sir. Not for a minute.

Any man who wants to get the votes of the Missinaba farmers and the Mariposa business men has got to persuade them that he's the right man. If he can do that, – if he can persuade any one of them that he is the right man and that all the rest know it, then they'll vote for him.

The division, I repeat, between the Liberals and the Conservatives, is intense. Yet you might live for a long while in the town, between elections, and never know it. It is only when you get to understand the people that you begin to see that there is a cross division running through them that nothing can ever remove. You gradually become aware of fine subtle distinctions that miss your observation at first. Outwardly, they are all friendly enough. For instance, Joe Milligan the dentist is a Conservative, and has been for six years, and yet he shares the same boathouse with young Dr. Gallagher, who is a Liberal, and they even bought a motor boat between them. Pete Glover and Alf McNichol were in partnership in the hardware and paint store, though they belonged on different sides.

But just as soon as elections drew near, the differences in politics became perfectly apparent. Liberals and Conservatives drew away from one another. Joe Milligan used the motor boat one Saturday and Dr. Gallagher the next, and Pete Glover sold hardware on one side of the store and Alf McNichol sold paint on the other. You soon realized too that one of the newspapers was Conservative and the other was Liberal, and that there was a Liberal drug store and a Conservative drug store, and so on. Similarly round election time, the Mariposa House was the Liberal Hotel, and the Continental, Conservative, though Mr. Smith's place, where they always put on a couple of extra bar tenders, was what you might call Independent-Liberal-Conservative, with a dash of Imperialism thrown in. Mr. Gingham, the undertaker, was, as a natural effect of his calling, an advanced Liberal, but at election time he always engaged a special assistant for embalming Conservative customers.

So now, I think, you understand something of the general political surroundings of the great election in Missinaba County.

John Henry Bagshaw was the sitting member, the Liberal member, for Missinaba County.

The Liberals called him the old war horse, and the old battle-axe, and the old charger and the old champion and all sorts of things of that kind. The Conservatives called him the old jackass and the old army mule and the old booze fighter and the old grafter and the old scoundrel.

John Henry Bagshaw was, I suppose, one of the greatest political forces in the world. He had flowing white hair crowned with a fedora hat, and a smooth statesmanlike face which it cost the country twenty-five cents a day to shave.

Altogether the Dominion of Canada had spent over two thousand dollars in shaving that face during the twenty years that Bagshaw had represented Missinaba County. But the result had been well worth it.

Bagshaw wore a long political overcoat that it cost the country twenty cents a day to brush, and boots that cost the Dominion fifteen cents every morning to shine.

But it was money well spent.

Bagshaw of Mariposa was one of the most representative men of the age, and it's no wonder that he had been returned for the county for five elections running, leaving the Conservatives nowhere. Just think how representative he was. He owned two hundred acres out on the Third Concession and kept two men working on it all the time to prove that he was a practical farmer. They sent in fat hogs to the Missinaba County Agricultural Exposition and the World's Fair every autumn, and Bagshaw himself stood beside the pig pens with the judges, and wore a pair of corduroy breeches and chewed a straw all afternoon. After that if any farmer thought that he was not properly represented in Parliament, it showed that he was an ass.

Bagshaw owned a half share in the harness business

and a quarter share in the tannery and that made him a business man. He paid for a pew in the Presbyterian Church and that represented religion in Parliament. He attended college for two sessions thirty years ago, and that represented education and kept him abreast with modern science, if not ahead of it. He kept a little account in one bank and a big account in the other, so that he was a rich man or a poor man at the same time.

Add to that that John Henry Bagshaw was perhaps the finest orator in Mariposa. That, of course, is saying a great deal. There are speakers there, lots of them that can talk two or three hours at a stretch, but the old war horse could beat them all. They say that when John Henry Bagshaw got well started, say after a couple of hours of talk, he could speak as Pericles or Demosthenes or Cicero never could have spoken.

You could tell Bagshaw a hundred yards off as a member of the House of Commons. He wore a pepper-and-salt suit to show that he came from a rural constituency, and he wore a broad gold watch-chain with dangling seals to show that he also represents a town. You could see from his quiet low collar and white tie that his electorate were a God-fearing, religious people, while the horseshoe pin that he wore showed that his electorate were not without sporting instincts and knew a horse from a jackass.

Most of the time, John Henry Bagshaw had to be at Ottawa (though he preferred the quiet of his farm and always left it, as he said, with a sigh). If he was not in Ottawa, he was in Washington, and of course at any time they might need him in London, so that it was no

MISSINABA COUNTY AGRICULTURAL EXPOSITION
AND WORLD'S FAIR

wonder that he could only be in Mariposa about two months of the year.

That is why everybody knew, when Bagshaw got off the afternoon train one day early in the spring, that there must be something very important coming and that the rumours about a new election must be perfectly true.

Everything that he did showed this. He gave the baggage man twenty-five cents to take the check off his trunk, the bus driver fifty cents to drive him up to the Main Street, and he went into Callahan's tobacco store and bought two ten-cent cigars and took them across the street and gave them to Mallory Tompkins of the Times-Herald as a present from the Prime Minister.

All that afternoon, Bagshaw went up and down the Main Street of Mariposa, and you could see, if you knew the signs of it, that there was politics in the air. He bought nails and putty and glass in the hardware store, and harness in the harness shop, and drugs in the drug store and toys in the toy shop, and all the things like that that are needed for a big campaign.

Then when he had done all this he went over with McGinnis the Liberal organizer and Mallory Tompkins, the Times-Herald man, and Gingham (the great Independent-Liberal undertaker) to the back parlour in the Mariposa House.

You could tell from the way John Henry Bagshaw closed the door before he sat down that he was in a pretty serious frame of mind.

"Gentlemen," he said, "the election is a certainty. We're going to have a big fight on our hands and we've got to get ready for it."

"Is it going to be on the tariff?" asked Tompkins.

"Yes, gentlemen, I'm afraid it is. The whole thing is going to turn on the tariff question. I wish it were otherwise. I think it madness, but they're bent on it, and we got to fight it on that line. Why they can't fight it merely on the question of graft," continued the old war horse, rising from his seat and walking up and down, "Heaven only knows. I warned them. I appealed to them. I said, fight the thing on graft and we can win easy. Take this constituency, – why not have fought the thing out on whether I spent too much money on the town wharf or the post-office? What better issues could a man want? Let them claim that I am crooked, and let me claim that I'm not. Surely that was good enough without dragging in the tariff. But now, gentlemen, tell me about things in the constituency. Is there any talk yet of who is to run?"

Mallory Tompkins lighted up the second of his Prime Minister's cigars and then answered for the group:

"Everybody says that Edward Drone is going to run."

"Ah!" said the old war horse, and there was joy upon his face, "is he? At last! That's good, that's good – now what platform will he run on?"

"Independent."

"Excellent," said Mr. Bagshaw. "Independent, that's fine. On a programme of what?"

"Just simple honesty and public morality."

"Come now," said the member, "that's splendid: that will help enormously. Honesty and public morality! The very thing! If Drone runs and makes a good showing, we win for a certainty. Tompkins, you must lose no time over this. Can't you manage to get some articles in the other papers hinting that at the last election we bribed all the voters in the county, and that we gave out enough contracts to simply pervert the whole constituency. Imply that we poured the public money into this county in bucketsful and that we are bound to do it again. Let Drone have plenty of material of this sort and he'll draw off every honest unbiassed vote in the Conservative party.

"My only fear is," continued the old war horse, losing some of his animation, "that Drone won't run after all. He's said it so often before and never has. He hasn't got the money. But we must see to that. Gingham, you know his brother well; you must work it so that we pay Drone's deposit and his campaign expenses. But how like Drone it is to come out at this time!"

It was indeed very like Edward Drone to attempt so misguided a thing as to come out an Independent candidate in Missinaba County on a platform of public honesty. It was just the sort of thing that anyone in Mariposa would expect from him.

Edward Drone was the Rural Dean's younger brother, – young Mr. Drone, they used to call him, years ago, to distinguish him from the rector. He was a somewhat weaker copy of his elder brother, with a simple, inefficient face and kind blue eyes. Edward Drone was, and always had been, a failure. In training he had been, once upon a time, an engineer and built dams that broke and bridges that fell down and wharves that floated away in the spring floods. He had been a manufacturer and failed, had been a contractor and failed, and now lived a meagre life as a sort of surveyor or land expert on goodness knows what.

In his political ideas Edward Drone was and, as everybody in Mariposa knew, always had been crazy. He used to come up to the autumn exercises at the high school and make speeches about the ancient Romans and Titus Manlius and Quintus Curtius at the same time when John Henry Bagshaw used to make a speech about the Maple Leaf and ask for an extra half holiday. Drone used to tell the boys about the lessons to be learned from the lives of the truly great, and Bagshaw used to talk to them about the lessons learned from the lives of the extremely rich. Drone used to say that his heart filled whenever he thought of the splendid patriotism of the ancient Romans, and Bagshaw said that whenever he looked out over this wide Dominion his heart overflowed.

Even the youngest boy in the school could tell that Drone was foolish. Not even the school teachers would have voted for him.

"What about the Conservatives?" asked Bagshaw presently; "is there any talk yet as to who they'll bring out?"

Gingham and Mallory Tompkins looked at one another. They were almost afraid to speak.

"Hadn't you heard?" said Gingham; "they've got their man already."

"Who is it?" said Bagshaw quickly.

"They're going to put up Josh Smith."

"Great Heaven!" said Bagshaw, jumping to his feet; "Smith! the hotel keeper."

"Yes, sir," said Mr. Gingham, "that's the man."

Do you remember, in history, how Napoleon turned pale when he heard that the Duke of Wellington was to lead the allies in Belgium? Do you remember how when Themistocles heard that Aristogiton was to lead the Spartans, he jumped into the sea? Possibly you don't, but it may help you to form some idea of what John Henry Bagshaw felt when he heard that the Conservatives had selected Josh Smith, proprietor of Smith's Hotel.

You remember Smith. You've seen him there on the steps of his hotel, – two hundred and eighty pounds in his stockinged feet. You've seen him selling liquor after hours through sheer public spirit, and you recall how he saved the lives of hundreds of people on the day when the steamer sank, and how he saved the town from being destroyed the night when the Church of England Church burnt down. You know that hotel of his, too, half way down the street, Smith's Northern Health Resort, though already they were beginning to call it Smith's British Arms.

So you can imagine that Bagshaw came as near to turning pale as a man in federal politics can.

"I never knew Smith was a Conservative," he said faintly; "he always subscribed to our fund."

"He is now," said Mr. Gingham ominously; "he says the idea of this reciprocity business cuts him to the heart."

"The infernal liar!" said Mr. Bagshaw.

There was silence for a few moments. Then Bagshaw spoke again.

"Will Smith have anything else in his platform besides the trade question?"

"Yes," said Mr. Gingham gloomily, "he will."

"What is it?"

"Temperance and total prohibition!"

John Henry Bagshaw sank back in his chair as if struck with a club. There let me leave him for a chapter.

POSTMASTER TRELAWNEY

# THE CANDIDACY OF MR. SMITH

"**B**oys," said Mr. Smith to the two hostlers, stepping out on to the sidewalk in front of the hotel, – "hoist that there British Jack over the place and hoist her up good."

Then he stood and watched the flag fluttering in the wind.

"Billy," he said to the desk clerk, "get a couple more and put them up on the roof of the caff behind the hotel. Wire down to the city and get a quotation on a hundred of them. Take them signs '*American Drinks*' out of the bar. Put up noo ones with '*British Beer at all Hours*'; clear out the rye whiskey and order in Scotch and Irish, and then go up to the printing office and get me them placards."

Then another thought struck Mr. Smith.

"Say, Billy," he said, "wire to the city for fifty pictures of King George. Get 'em good, and get 'em coloured. It don't matter what they cost."

"All right, sir," said Billy.

"And Billy," called Mr. Smith, as still another thought struck him (indeed, the moment Mr. Smith went into politics you could see these thoughts strike him like waves), get fifty pictures of his father, old King Albert. "

"All right, sir."

"And say, I tell you, while you're at it, get some of the old queen, Victorina, if you can. Get 'em in mourning, with a harp and one of them lions and a three-pointed prong."

It was on the morning after the Conservative Convention. Josh Smith had been chosen the candidate. And now the whole town was covered with flags and placards and there were bands in the streets every evening, and noise and music and excitement that went on from morning till night.

Election times are exciting enough even in the city. But there the excitement dies down in business hours. In Mariposa there aren't any business hours and the excitement goes on *all* the time.

Mr. Smith had carried the Convention before him. There had been a feeble attempt to put up Nivens. But everybody knew that he was a lawyer and a college man and wouldn't have a chance by a man with a broader outlook like Josh Smith.

So the result was that Smith was the candidate and there were placards out all over the town with SMITH AND BRITISH ALLEGIANCE in big letters, and people were wearing badges with Mr. Smith's face on one side and King George's on the other, and the fruit store next to the hotel had been cleaned out and turned into committee rooms with a gang of workers smoking cigars in it all day and half the night.

There were other placards, too, with BAGSHAW AND LIBERTY, BAGSHAW AND PROSPERITY, VOTE FOR THE OLD

MISSINABA STANDARD BEARER, and up town beside the Mariposa House there were the Bagshaw committee rooms with a huge white streamer across the street, and with a gang of Bagshaw workers smoking their heads off.

But Mr. Smith had an estimate made which showed that nearly two cigars to one were smoked in his committee rooms as compared with the Liberals. It was the first time in five elections that the Conservative had been able to make such a showing as that.

One might mention, too, that there were Drone placards out, – five or six of them, – little things about the size of a pocket handkerchief, with a statement that "Mr. Edward Drone solicits the votes of the electors of Missinaba County." But you would never notice them. And when Drone tried to put up a streamer across the Main Street with DRONE AND HONESTY the wind carried it away into the lake.

The fight was really between Smith and Bagshaw, and everybody knew it from the start.

I wish that I were able to narrate all the phases and the turns of the great contest from the opening of the campaign till the final polling day. But it would take volumes.

First of all, of course, the trade question was hotly discussed in the two newspapers of Mariposa, and the Newspacket and the Times-Herald literally bristled with statistics. Then came interviews with the candidates and the expression of their convictions in regard to tariff questions.

"Mr. Smith," said the reporter of the Mariposa Newspacket, "we'd like to get your views of the effect of the proposed reduction of the differential duties."

"By gosh, Pete," said Mr. Smith, "you can search me. Have a cigar."

"What do you think, Mr. Smith, would be the result of lowering the *ad valorem* British preference and admitting American goods at a reciprocal rate?"

"It's a corker, ain't it?" answered Mr. Smith. "What'll you take, lager or domestic?"

And in that short dialogue Mr. Smith showed that he had instantaneously grasped the whole method of dealing with the press. The interview in the paper next day said that Mr. Smith, while unwilling to state positively that the principle of tariff discrimination was at variance with sound fiscal science, was firmly of opinion that any reciprocal interchange of tariff preferences with the United States must inevitably lead to a serious per capita reduction of the national industry.

"Mr. Smith," said the chairman of a delegation of the manufacturers of Mariposa, "what do you propose to do in regard to the tariff if you're elected?"

"Boys," answered Mr. Smith, "I'll put her up so darned high they won't never get her down again."

"Mr. Smith," said the chairman of another delegation, "I'm an old free trader –"

"Put it there," said Mr. Smith, "so'm I. There ain't nothing like it."

"What do you think about imperial defence?" asked another questioner.

"Which?" said Mr. Smith.

"Imperial defence."

"Of what?"

"Of everything."

"Who says it?" said Mr. Smith.

"Everybody is talking of it."

"What do the Conservative boys at Ottaway think about it?" answered Mr. Smith.

"They're all for it."

"Well, I'm fer it too," said Mr. Smith.

These little conversations represented only the first stage, the argumentative stage of the great contest. It was during this period, for example, that the Mariposa Newspacket absolutely proved that the price of hogs in Mariposa was decimal six higher than the price of oranges in Southern California and that the average decennial import of eggs into Missinaba County had increased four decimal six eight two in the last fifteen years more than the import of lemons in New Orleans.

Figures of this kind made the people think. Most certainly.

After all this came the organizing stage and after that the big public meetings and the rallies. Perhaps you have never seen a county being "organized." It is a wonderful sight. First of all the Bagshaw men drove through crosswise in top buggies and then drove through it again lengthwise. Whenever they met a farmer they went in and ate a meal with him, and after the meal they took him out to the buggy and gave him a drink. After that the man's vote was absolutely solid until it was tampered with by feeding a Conservative.

In fact, the only way to show a farmer that you are in earnest is to go in and eat a meal with him. If you won't eat it, he won't vote for you. That is the recognized political test.

But, of course, just as soon as the Bagshaw men had begun to get the farming vote solidified, the Smith buggies came driving through in the other direction, eating meals and distributing cigars and turning all the farmers back into Conservatives.

Here and there you might see Edward Drone, the Independent candidate, wandering round from farm to farm in the dust of the political buggies. To each of the farmers he explained that he pledged himself to give no bribes, to spend no money and to offer no jobs, and each one of them gripped him warmly by the hand and showed him the way to the next farm.

After the organization of the county there came the period of the public meetings and the rallies and the joint debates between the candidates and their supporters.

I suppose there was no place in the whole Dominion where the trade question – the Reciprocity question – was threshed out quite so thoroughly and in quite such a national patriotic spirit as in Mariposa. For a month, at least, people talked of nothing else. A man would stop another in the street and tell him that he had read last night that the average price of an egg in New York was decimal ought one more than the price of an egg in Mariposa, and the other man would stop the first one later in the day and tell him that the average price of a hog in Idaho was point six of a cent per pound less (or more, – he couldn't remember which for the moment) than the average price of beef in Mariposa.

People lived on figures of this sort, and the man who could remember most of them stood out as a born leader.

But of course it was at the public meetings that these things were most fully discussed. It would take volumes to do full justice to all the meetings that they held in Missinaba County. But here and there single speeches stood out as masterpieces of convincing oratory. Take, for example, the speech of John Henry Bagshaw at the Tecumseh Corners School House. The Mariposa Times-Herald said next day that that speech would go down in history, and so it will, – ever so far down.

Anyone who has heard Bagshaw knows what an impressive speaker he is, and on this night when he spoke with the quiet dignity of a man old in years and anxious only to serve his country, he almost surpassed himself. Near the end of his speech somebody dropped a pin, and the noise it made in falling fairly rattled the windows.

"I am an old man now, gentlemen," Bagshaw said, "and the time must soon come when I must not only leave politics, but must take my way towards that goal from which no traveller returns."

There was a deep hush when Bagshaw said this. It was understood to imply that he thought of going to the United States.

"Yes, gentlemen, I am an old man, and I wish, when my time comes to go, to depart leaving as little animosity behind me as possible. But before I *do* go, I want it pretty clearly understood that there are more darn scoundrels in the Conservative party than ought to be tolerated in any decent community. I bear," he continued, "malice towards none and I wish to speak with gentleness to all, but what I will say is that how any set of rational responsible men could nominate such a skunk as the Conservative candidate passes the bounds of my comprehension. Gentlemen, in the present campaign there is no room for vindictive abuse. Let us rise to a higher level than that. They tell me that my opponent, Smith, is a common saloon keeper. Let it pass. They tell me that he has stood convicted of horse stealing, that he is a notable perjurer, that he is known as the blackest-hearted liar in Missinaba County. Let us not speak of it. Let no whisper of it pass our lips.

"No, gentlemen," continued Bagshaw, pausing to take a drink of water, "let us rather consider this question on the high plane of national welfare. Let us not think of our own particular interests but let us consider the good of the country at large. And to do this, let me present to you some facts in regard to the price of barley in Tecumseh Township."

Then, amid a deep stillness, Bagshaw read off the list of prices of sixteen kinds of grain in sixteen different places during sixteen years.

"But let me turn," Bagshaw went on to another phase of the national subject, "and view for a moment the price of marsh hay in Missinaba County –"

When Bagshaw sat down that night it was felt that a Liberal vote in Tecumseh Township was a foregone conclusion.

But here they hadn't reckoned on the political genius of Mr. Smith. When he heard next day of the meeting, he summoned some of his leading speakers to him and he said:

"Boys, they're beating us on them statissicks. Ourn ain't good enough."

Then he turned to Nivens and he said:

"What was them figures you had here the other night?"

Nivens took out a paper and began reading.

"Stop," said Mr. Smith, "what was that figure for bacon?"

"Fourteen million dollars," said Nivens.

"Not enough," said Mr. Smith, "make it twenty. They'll stand for it, them farmers."

Nivens changed it.

"And what was that for hay?"

"Two dollars a ton."

"Shove it up to four," said Mr. Smith. "And I tell you," he added, "if any of them farmers says the figures ain't correct, tell them to go to Washington and see for themselves; say that if any man wants the proof of your figures let him go over to England and ask, – tell him to go straight to London and see it all for himself in the books."

After this, there was no more trouble over statistics. I must say though that it is a wonderfully convincing thing to hear trade figures of this kind properly handled. Perhaps the best man on this sort of thing in the campaign was Mullins, the banker. A man of his profession simply has to have figures of trade and population and money at his fingers' ends and the effect of it in public speaking is wonderful.

No doubt you have listened to speakers of this kind, but I question whether you have ever heard anything more typical of the sort of effect that I allude to than Mullins's speech at the big rally at the Fourth Concession.

Mullins himself, of course, knows the figures so well that he never bothers to write them into notes and the effect is very striking.

"Now, gentlemen," he said very earnestly, "how many of you know just to what extent the exports of this country have increased in the last ten years? How many could tell what per cent of increase there has been in one decade of our national importation?" – then Mullins paused and looked round. Not a man knew it.

"I don't recall," he said, "exactly the precise amount myself, – not at this moment, – but it must be simply tremendous. Or take the question of popula-tion," Mullins went on, warming up again as a born statistician always does at the proximity of figures, "how many of you know, how many of you can state, what has been the decennial percentage increase in our leading cities –?"

There he paused, and would you believe it, not a man could state it.

"I don't recall the exact figures," said Mullins, "but I have them at home and they are positively colossal."

But just in one phase of the public speaking, the can-didacy of Mr. Smith received a serious set-back.

It had been arranged that Mr. Smith should run on a platform of total prohibition. But they soon found that it was a mistake. They had imported a special speaker from the city, a grave man with a white tie, who put his whole heart into the work and would take nothing for it except his expenses and a sum of money for each speech. But beyond the money, I say, he would take nothing.

He spoke one night at the Tecumseh Corners social hall at the same time when the Liberal meeting was going on at the Tecumseh Corners school house.

"Gentlemen," he said, as he paused half way in his speech, – "while we are gathered here in earnest discussion, do you know what is happening over at the meeting place of our opponents? Do you know that seventeen bottles of rye whiskey were sent out from the town this afternoon to that innocent and unsuspecting school house? Seventeen bottles of whiskey hidden in between the blackboard and the wall, and every single man that attends that meeting, – mark my words, every single man, – will drink his fill of the abominable stuff at the expense of the Liberal candidate!"

Just as soon as the speaker said this, you could see the Smith men at the meeting look at one another in injured surprise, and before the speech was half over the hall was practically emptied.

After that the total prohibition plank was changed and the committee substituted a declaration in favour of such a form of restrictive license as should promote temperance while encouraging the manufacture of spirituous liquors, and by a severe regulation of the liquor traffic should place intoxicants only in the hands of those fitted to use them.

Finally there came the great day itself, the Election Day that brought, as everybody knows, the crowning triumph of Mr. Smith's career. There is no need to speak of it at

any length, because it has become a matter of history.

In any case, everybody who has ever seen Mariposa knows just what election day is like. The shops, of course, are, as a matter of custom, all closed, and the bar rooms are all closed by law so that you have to go in by the back way. All the people are in their best clothes and at first they walk up and down the street in a solemn way just as they do on the twelfth of July and on St. Patrick's Day, before the fun begins. Everybody keeps looking in at the different polling places to see if anybody else has voted yet, because, of course, nobody cares to vote first for fear of being fooled after all and voting on the wrong side.

Most of all did the supporters of Mr. Smith, acting under his instructions, hang back from the poll in the early hours. To Mr. Smith's mind, voting was to be conducted on the same plan as bear-shooting.

"Hold back your votes, boys," he said, "and don't be too eager. Wait till she begins to warm up and then let 'em have it good and hard."

In each of the polling places in Mariposa there is a returning officer and with him are two scrutineers, and the electors, I say, peep in and out like mice looking into a trap. But if once the scrutineers get a man well into the polling booth, they push him in behind a little curtain and make him vote. The voting, of course, is by secret ballot, so that no one except the scrutineers and the returning officer and the two or three people who may be round the poll can possibly tell how a man has voted.

That's how it comes about that the first results are often so contradictory and conflicting. Sometimes the poll is badly arranged and the scrutineers are unable to see properly just how the ballots are being marked and they count up the Liberals and Conservatives in different ways. Often, too, a voter makes his mark so hurriedly and carelessly that they have to pick it out of the ballot box and look at it to see what it is.

I suppose that may have been why it was that in Mariposa the results came out at first in such a conflicting way.

Perhaps that was how it was that the first reports showed that Edward Drone the Independent candidate was certain to win. You should have seen how the excitement grew upon the streets when the news was circulated. In the big rallies and meetings of the Liberals and Conservatives, everybody had pretty well forgotten all about Drone, and when the news got round at about four o'clock that the Drone vote was carrying the poll, the people were simply astounded. Not that they were not pleased. On the contrary. They were delighted. Everybody came up to Drone and shook hands and congratulated him and told him that they had known all along that what the country wanted was a straight, honest, non-partisan representation. The Conservatives said openly that they were sick of party, utterly done with it, and the Liberals said that they hated it. Already three or four of them had taken Drone aside and explained that what was needed in the town was a straight, clean, non-partisan post-office, built on a piece of ground of a strictly non-partisan character, and constructed under contracts that were not tainted and smirched with party affiliation. Two or three men were willing to show to Drone just where a piece of ground of this character could be bought. They told him too that in the matter of the postmastership itself they had nothing against Trelawney, the present post-master, in any personal sense, and would say nothing against him except merely that he was utterly and hopelessly unfit for his job and that if Drone believed, as he had said he did, in a purified civil service, he ought to begin by purifying Trelawney.

Already Edward Drone was beginning to feel something of what it meant to hold office and there was creeping into his manner the quiet self-importance which is the first sign of conscious power.

In fact, in that brief half-hour of office, Drone had a chance to see something of what it meant. Henry McGinnis came to him and asked straight out for a job as federal census-taker on the ground that he was hard up and had been crippled with rheumatism all winter. Nelson Williamson asked for the post of wharf master on the plea that he had been laid up with sciatica all winter and was absolutely fit for nothing. Erasmus Archer asked him if he could get his boy Pete into one of the departments at Ottawa, and made a strong case of it by explaining that he had tried his cussedest to get Pete a job anywhere else and it was simply impossible. Not that Pete wasn't a willing boy, but he was slow, – even his father admitted it, – slow as the devil, blast him, and with no head for figures and unfortunately he'd never had the schooling to bring him on. But if Drone could get him in at Ottawa, his father truly believed it would be the very place for him. Surely in the Indian Department or in the Astronomical Branch or in the New Canadian

Navy there must be any amount of openings for a boy like this? And to all of these requests Drone found himself explaining that he would take the matter under his very earnest consideration and that they must remember that he had to consult his colleagues and not merely follow the dictates of his own wishes. In fact, if he had ever in his life had any envy of Cabinet Ministers, he lost it in this hour.

But Drone's hour was short. Even before the poll had closed in Mariposa, the news came sweeping in, true or false, that Bagshaw was carrying the county. The second concession had gone for Bagshaw in a regular landslide, – six votes to only two for Smith, – and all down the township line road (where the hay farms are) Bagshaw was said to be carrying all before him.

Just as soon as that news went round the town, they launched the Mariposa band of the Knights of Pythias (every man in it is a Liberal) down the Main Street with big red banners in front of it with the motto BAGSHAW FOREVER in letters a foot high. Such rejoicing and enthusiasm began to set in as you never saw. Everybody crowded round Bagshaw on the steps of the Mariposa House and shook his hand and said they were proud to see the day and that the Liberal party was the glory of the Dominion and that as for this idea of non-partisan politics the very thought of it made them sick. Right away in the committee rooms they began to organize the demonstration for the evening with lantern slides and speeches and they arranged for a huge bouquet to be presented to Bagshaw on the platform by four little girls (all Liberals) all dressed in white.

And it was just at this juncture, with one hour of voting left, that Mr. Smith emerged from his committee rooms and turned his voters on the town, much as the Duke of Wellington sent the whole line to the charge at Waterloo. From every committee room and sub-committee room they poured out in flocks with blue badges fluttering on their coats.

"Get at it, boys," said Mr. Smith, "vote and keep on voting till they make you quit."

Then he turned to his campaign assistant. "Billy," he said, "wire down to the city that I'm elected by an over-whelming majority and tell them to wire it right back. Send word by telephone to all the polling places in the county that the hull town has gone solid Conservative and tell them to send the same news back here. Get carpenters and tell them to run up a platform in front of the hotel; tell them to take the bar door clean off its hinges and be all ready the minute the poll quits."

It was that last hour that did it. Just as soon as the big posters went up in the windows of the Mariposa Newspacket with the telegraphic despatch that Josh Smith was reported in the city to be elected, and was followed by the messages from all over the county, the voters hesitated no longer. They had waited, most of them, all through the day, not wanting to make any error in their vote, but when they saw the Smith men crowding into the polls and heard the news from the outside, they went solid in one great stampede, and by the time the poll was declared closed at five o'clock there was no shadow of doubt that the county was saved and that Josh Smith was elected for Missinaba.

---

I wish you could have witnessed the scene in Mariposa that evening. It would have done your heart good, – such joy, such public rejoicing as you never saw. It turned out that there wasn't really a Liberal in the whole town and that there never had been. They were all Conservatives and had been for years and years. Men who had voted, with pain and sorrow in their hearts, for the Liberal party for twenty years, came out that evening and owned up straight that they were Conservatives. They said they could stand the strain no longer and simply had to confess. Whatever the sacrifice might mean, they were prepared to make it.

Even Mr. Golgotha Gingham, the undertaker, came out and admitted that in working for John Henry Bagshaw he'd been going straight against his conscience. He said that right from the first he had had his misgivings. He said it had haunted him. Often at night when he would be working away quietly, one of these sudden misgivings would overcome him so that he could hardly go on with his embalming. Why, it appeared that on the very first day when reciprocity was proposed, he had come home and said to Mrs. Gingham that he thought it simply meant selling out the country. And the strange thing was that ever so many others had just the same misgivings. Trelawney admitted that he had said to Mrs. Trelawney that it was madness, and Jeff Thorpe, the barber, had, he admitted, gone home to his dinner, the first day reciprocity was talked of, and said to Mrs. Thorpe that it would simply kill business in the country and introduce a cheap, shoddy, American form of haircut that would render true loyalty impossible. To think that Mrs. Gingham and

Mrs. Trelawney and Mrs. Thorpe had known all this for six months and kept quiet about it! Yet I think there were a good many Mrs. Ginghams in the country. It is merely another proof that no woman is fit for politics.

The demonstration that night in Mariposa will never be forgotten. The excitement in the streets, the torchlights, the music of the band of the Knights of Pythias (an organization which is conservative in all but name), and above all the speeches and the patriotism.

They had put up a big platform in front of the hotel, and on it were Mr. Smith and his chief workers, and behind them was a perfect forest of flags. They presented a huge bouquet of flowers to Mr. Smith, handed to him by four little girls in white, – the same four that I spoke of above, for it turned out that they were all Conservatives.

Then there were the speeches. Judge Pepperleigh spoke and said that there was no need to dwell on the victory that they had achieved, because it was history; there was no occasion to speak of what part he himself had played, within the limits of his official position, because what he had done was henceforth a matter of history; and Nivens, the lawyer, said that he would only say just a few words, because anything that he might have done was now history; later generations, he said, might read it but it was not for him to speak of it, because it belonged now to the history of the country. And, after them, others spoke in the same strain and all refused absolutely to dwell on the subject (for more than half an hour) on the ground that anything that they might have done was better left for future generations to investigate. And no doubt this was very true, as to some things, anyway.

Mr. Smith, of course, said nothing. He didn't have to, – not for four years, – and he knew it.

# L'ENVOI.
# THE TRAIN TO
# MARIPOSA

IT LEAVES THE CITY every day about five o'clock in the evening, the train for Mariposa.

Strange that you did not know of it, though you come from the little town – or did, long years ago.

Odd that you never knew, in all these years, that the train was there every afternoon, puffing up steam in the city station, and that you might have boarded it any day and gone home. No, not "home," – of course you couldn't call it "home" now; "home" means that big red sandstone house of yours in the costlier part of the city. "Home" means, in a way, this Mausoleum Club where you sometimes talk with me of the times that you had as a boy in Mariposa.

But of course "home" would hardly be the word you would apply to the little town, unless perhaps, late at night, when you'd been sitting reading in a quiet corner somewhere such a book as the present one.

Naturally you don't know of the Mariposa train now. Years ago, when you first came to the city as a boy with your way to make, you knew of it well enough, only too well. The price of a ticket counted in those days, and though you knew of the train you couldn't take it, but sometimes from sheer homesickness you used to wander down to the station on a Friday afternoon after your work, and watch the Mariposa people getting on the train and wish that you could go.

Why, you knew that train at one time better, I suppose, than any other single thing in the city, and loved it too for the little town in the sunshine that it ran to.

Do you remember how when you first began to make money you used to plan that just as soon as you were rich, really rich, you'd go back home again to the little town and build a great big house with a fine verandah, – no stint about it, the best that money could buy, planed lumber, every square foot of it, and a fine picket fence in front of it.

It was to be one of the grandest and finest houses that thought could conceive; much finer, in true reality, than that vast palace of sandstone with the porte cochère and the sweeping conservatories that you afterwards built in the costlier part of the city.

But if you have half forgotten Mariposa, and long since lost the way to it, you are only like the greater part of the men here in this Mausoleum Club in the city. Would you believe it that practically every one of them came from Mariposa once upon a time, and that there isn't one of them that doesn't sometimes dream in the dull quiet of the long evening here in the club, that some day he will go back and see the place.

They all do. Only they're half ashamed to own it.

Ask your neighbour there at the next table whether the partridge that they sometimes serve to you here can be compared for a moment to the birds that he and you, or he and some one else, used to shoot as boys in the spruce thickets along the lake. Ask him if he ever tasted duck that could for a moment be compared to the black ducks in the rice marsh along the Ossawippi. And as for fish, and fishing, – no, don't ask him about that, for if he ever starts telling you of the chub they used to catch below the mill dam and the green bass that used to lie in the water-shadow of the rocks beside the Indian's Island, not even the long dull evening in this club would be long enough for the telling of it.

But no wonder they don't know about the five o'clock train for Mariposa. Very few people know about it. Hundreds of them know that there is a train that goes out at five o'clock, but they mistake it. Ever so many of them think it's just a suburban train. Lots of people that take it every day think it's only the train to the golf grounds, but the joke is that after it passes out of the city and the suburbs and the golf grounds, it turns itself little by little into the Mariposa train, thundering and pounding towards the north with hemlock sparks pouring out into the darkness from the funnel of it.

Of course you can't tell it just at first. All those people that are crowding into it with golf clubs, and wearing knickerbockers and flat caps, would deceive anybody. That crowd of suburban people going home on commutation tickets and sometimes standing thick in the aisles, those are, of course, not Mariposa people. But look round a little bit and you'll find them easily enough.

Here and there in the crowd those people with the clothes that are perfectly all right and yet look odd in some way, the women with the peculiar hats and the – what do you say? – last year's fashions? Ah yes, of course, that must be it.

Anyway, those are the Mariposa people all right enough. That man with the two-dollar panama and the glaring spectacles is one of the greatest judges that ever adorned the bench of Missinaba County. That clerical gentleman with the wide black hat, who is explaining to the man with him the marvellous mechanism of the new air brake (one of the most conspicuous illustrations of the divine structure of the physical universe), surely you have seen him before. Mariposa people! Oh yes, there are any number of them on the train every day.

But of course you hardly recognize them while the train is still passing through the suburbs and the golf district and the outlying parts of the city area. But wait a little, and you will see that when the city is well behind you, bit by bit the train changes its character. The electric locomotive that took you through the city tunnels is off now and the old wood engine is hitched on in its place. I suppose, very probably, you haven't seen one of these wood engines since you were a boy forty years ago, – the old engine with a wide top like a hat on its funnel, and with sparks enough to light up a suit for damages once in every mile.

Do you see, too, that the trim little cars that came out of the city on the electric suburban express are being discarded now at the way stations, one by one, and in their place is the old familiar car with the stuff cushions in red plush (how gorgeous it once seemed!) and with a box stove set up in one end of it? The stove is burning furiously at its sticks this autumn evening, for the air sets in chill as you get clear away from the city and are rising up to the higher ground of the country of the pines and the lakes.

Look from the window as you go. The city is far behind now and right and left of you there are trim farms with elms and maples near them and with tall windmills beside the barns that you can still see in the gathering dusk. There is a dull red light from the windows of the farmstead. It must be comfortable there after the roar and clatter of the city, and only think of the still quiet of it.

As you sit back half dreaming in the car, you keep wondering why it is that you never came up before in all these years. Ever so many times you planned that just as soon as the rush and strain of business eased up a little, you would take the train and go back to the little town to see what it was like now, and if things had changed much since your day. But each time when your holidays came, somehow you changed your mind and went down to Naragansett or Nagahuckett or Nagasomething, and left over the visit to Mariposa for another time.

It is almost night now. You can still see the trees and the fences and the farmsteads, but they are fading fast in the twilight. They have lengthened out the train by this time with a string of flat cars and freight cars between where we are sitting and the engine. But at every crossway we can hear the long muffled roar of the whistle, dying to a melancholy wail that echoes into the woods; the woods, I say, for the farms are thinning out and the track plunges here and there into great stretches of bush, – tall tamarack and red scrub willow and with a tangled undergrowth of bush that has defied for two generations all attempts to clear it into the form of fields.

Why, look, that great space that seems to open out in the half-dark of the falling evening, – why, surely yes, – Lake Ossawippi, the big lake, as they used to call it, from which the river runs down to the smaller lake, – Lake Wissanotti, – where the town of Mariposa has lain waiting for you there for thirty years.

This is Lake Ossawippi surely enough. You would know it anywhere by the broad, still, black water with hardly a ripple, and with the grip of the coming frost already on it. Such a great sheet of blackness it looks as the train thunders along the side, swinging the curve of the embankment at a breakneck speed as it rounds the corner of the lake.

How fast the train goes this autumn night! You have travelled, I know you have; in the Empire State Express, and the New Limited and the Maritime Express that holds the record of six hundred whirling miles from Paris to Marseilles. But what are they to this, this mad career, this breakneck speed, this thundering roar of the Mariposa local driving hard to its home! Don't tell me that the speed is only twenty-five miles an hour. I don't care what it is. I tell you, and you can prove it for yourself if you will, that that train of mingled flat cars and coaches that goes tearing into the night, its engine whistle shrieking out its warning into the silent woods and echoing over the dull still lake, is the fastest train in the whole world.

Yes, and the best too, – the most comfortable, the

most reliable, the most luxurious and the speediest train that ever turned a wheel.

And the most genial, the most sociable too. See how the passengers all turn and talk to one another now as they get nearer and nearer to the little town. That dull reserve that seemed to hold the passengers in the electric suburban has clean vanished and gone. They are talking, – listen, – of the harvest, and the late election, and of how the local member is mentioned for the cabinet and all the old familiar topics of the sort. Already the conductor has changed his glazed hat for an ordinary round Christie and you can hear the passengers calling him and the brakesman "Bill" and "Sam" as if they were all one family.

What is it now – nine thirty? Ah, then we must be nearing the town, – this big bush that we are passing through, you remember it surely as the great swamp just this side of the bridge over the Ossawippi? There is the bridge itself, and the long roar of the train as it rushes sounding over the trestle work that rises above the marsh. Hear the clatter as we pass the semaphores and switch lights! We must be close in now!

What? it feels nervous and strange to be coming here again after all these years? It must indeed. No, don't bother to look at the reflection of your face in the window-pane shadowed by the night outside. Nobody could tell you now after all these years. Your face has changed in these long years of money-getting in the city. Perhaps if you had come back now and again, just at odd times, it wouldn't have been so.

There, – you hear it? – the long whistle of the locomotive, one, two, three! You feel the sharp slackening of the train as it swings round the curve of the last embankment that brings it to the Mariposa station. See, too, as we round the curve, the row of the flashing lights, the bright windows of the depôt.

How vivid and plain it all is. Just as it used to be thirty years ago. There is the string of the hotel buses, drawn up all ready for the train, and as the train rounds in and stops hissing and panting at the platform, you can hear above all other sounds the cry of the brakesmen and the porters:

"MARIPOSA! MARIPOSA!"

And as we listen, the cry grows fainter and fainter in our ears and we are sitting here again in the leather chairs of the Mausoleum Club, talking of the little Town in the Sunshine that once we knew.

# AFTERWORD

IF MY MEMORY can be trusted, then Stephen Leacock was the first author whose name I took notice of. This would have been when I was very young. It wasn't for any precocious reasons. It was entirely a case of mistaken identity.

I'm sure this odd mix-up wouldn't even have occurred if it wasn't for the fact that I was born in Clinton, Ontario, and so when I first encountered Stephen Leacock's name on the cover of a book, I strangely confused it with the name of a previous Clinton resident, Steven Truscott. Truscott, if you recall, was the teenage boy who had been falsely convicted of the terrible murder of Lynne Harper in my hometown back in the late 1950s (a few years before I was born). His name was often spoken in our little town.

I remember looking at the yellow cover of the New Canadian Library edition of *Sunshine Sketches of a Little Town* (I still remember the book) and wondering what this supposed murderer's book was all about. What was this little town he was writing of? Was it our town? And why was it so sunny there? His situation didn't strike me as too "sunny," and I couldn't puzzle out an answer, but, predictably, the oddness of the pairing kept Leacock's name alive in my mind.

And here is the strange part: my confusing Stephen Leacock with Steven Truscott wasn't as meaningless as it might initially seem. I think the mix-up helped me to eventually recognize the shadow that hangs over the sunny streets of Mariposa. Those quiet little Ontario towns are rarely as tranquil and bucolic as we'd like to imagine. There is usually something unpleasant or nasty hidden behind those doors and faded storefronts. Certainly the Clinton of my youth had a shadow over it. I felt it even before I knew the grim details, and I was aware of it long before I could fully appreciate what those details *really* meant.

Nothing quite so tragic sits at the heart of Mariposa, yet there is a surprising interplay of light and darkness in the book that is recognizable to anyone who has lived in a small town. I may not have picked up on this on my first reading, but as I have returned to the book over the years, I've come to appreciate the shadows in Mariposa as much as the sunshine.

I didn't read *Sunshine Sketches* until I was a teenager. I wasn't forced to read it like many school children are; I sought it out on my own. My early mix-up had made the book mysterious to me. Even the title was perplexing. I didn't understand why the word "sketches" was used. What kind of sketches were involved? My edition certainly wasn't illustrated! And I still wasn't too sure why these sketches were supposed to be so terribly sunny. In fact, thinking about it today, that title – with its queer nineteen-oh-something–era sound – might be the most dated aspect of the entire book.

That said, I liked it on the first read and found it quite engaging and surprisingly funny. This is more of a compliment than it sounds. My teenage tastes ran more toward Jack Kirby and *Heavy Metal* magazine than witty social satire.

When I read it again a few years later in my early twenties, I found it even funnier. It struck a deeper chord in me this time around, too. Maybe it was because, by then, I had moved away from the little towns of my childhood and was living in the big city of Toronto. I had just enough distance and years under my belt to *start* to appreciate what Leacock was skewering. Yes, the characters and the situations were still straightforwardly funny to me, but I was beginning to recognize the harder points of his humour – the dry tone, the wink of superiority, the delightful meanness of so much of it. I believe I once read that the residents of Orillia (the real Mariposa) weren't very flattered by the depiction of their little town in the book. I'm not surprised. It's not a flattering portrait of small-town life.

Back then, in the late 1980s, I was seriously falling in love with *The New Yorker* cartoonists of the 1920s to the 1950s, and was desperately scouring the dusty and depressing humour sections of Toronto's second-hand bookstores for any of the old *New Yorker* cartoon collections. Eventually my tastes broadened and I picked up the books of *The New Yorker* writers as well, including

James Thurber, E.B. White, Robert Benchley, Ring Lardner, and Wolcott Gibbs. I recall feeling a swell of national pride that these writers often listed Leacock as a beloved influence. I started noticing his other books in these humour sections as well. They were funny too, and often I laughed out loud while reading them. I still think that's high praise for a very old joke book!

But to be honest, those other Leacock books haven't stuck with me the way *Sunshine Sketches* has. Boiled down, I'd say that I'm a *Sunshine Sketches* enthusiast, but not necessarily a Leacock fan. *Sunshine Sketches* is his masterpiece. It's among a very small handful of favourite books that I return to again and again.

Why do I like it so? Well, it's not just because it's funny. I think I would like the book just as much even if it were half as funny. Primarily, I'm drawn to something else in it: how can I describe it? "Completeness," perhaps, or a sense of place. Leacock gives us a full little world that has been "mapped" out for us. Mariposa is introduced leisurely: first the hotel, then the barbershop, then the docks, the rectory, the church, and so on. All the while we are introduced either formally or casually to the town's residents, some important to the story, some incidental. By the time we close the book, we have experienced Mariposa as if some kind citizen had recognized us for a visitor, taken us by the arm, and given us a relaxed and gossipy guided tour.

It's the same reason why I like Sherwood Anderson's *Winesburg, Ohio* and Daniel Clowes's *Ice Haven* and Ludwig Bemelmans's *Hotel Splendide* and Kenneth Grahame's *The Wind in the Willows*. It's one of the reasons why I respond deeply to Margaret Laurence's Manawaka – and maybe even Alice Munro's southwestern Ontario (though that might be stretching it). It's probably why I so enjoyed the radio series *The Great Eastern*.

For me, it's more about the experience of coming to really *know* a fictional locality rather than simply discovering the particularities of the story or its characters. There is something very satisfying about becoming fully acquainted with an imaginary place. I feel like I have walked Mariposa's elm-lined streets. I recognize its tavern and its drugstore and its grand church. I've seen such landmarks linger on in many small towns across Ontario. This sense of place is certainly one of the big reasons why I like the old-time Canadian comic strip *Birdseye Center* by Jimmy Frise (set in yet another small town). I even tried to put a bit of Jimmy's folksy, big-foot-and-rubber-nosed drawing style into this edition. Jimmy's *Birdseye Center* and Leacock's Mariposa seem as though they might only be a few miles apart. Linking them – even if it is with just a few stylistic "licks" – somehow feels right to me.

Still, I wouldn't want to reduce the entire appeal of the book to "world building." You don't create a lasting work of art simply with good cataloging skills. *Sunshine Sketches* is smart and funny and very, very sophisticated. It is the work of a clever, complicated man.

I mentioned earlier the yellow cover of that New Canadian Library edition I saw as a child. The yellowness stuck in my mind too. In a sort of synesthetic manner, I've always detected a kind of "yellow" note in Leacock's writing – not quite sour, nor quite sunshiny. It's not purely funny nor straightforwardly satiric. Not simply mean either: there's too much love in it for that, and yet not enough love to be truly sympathetic. Leacock likes the people of Mariposa well enough, but that doesn't prevent him from looking down his nose at them. He certainly doesn't refrain from pointing out their shortcomings.

It's a curious fact that his "sketches" are among the harshest portraits of "just folk" around, and yet somehow, inexplicably, you close the book feeling genuine affection for these sometimes selfish, often foolish, always naive small-town inhabitants. Why is that? I'm not entirely sure, but, undoubtedly, it's a large part of the book's mystique. Some touch of genuine observation, some real feeling, some sharp edge raises it above the danger of being merely a humorous distraction.

And finally, there is that marvellous otherworldly closing chapter. That hypnotic train ride into the night and backward in time. It's my favourite thing about the book. A chapter strangely out of tone with the rest of the work – deeply melancholic, nostalgic even, filled with longing for the places of our origins, for that which is out of reach.

How does Leacock manage to impart such warm emotions after he has devoted so many pages to showcasing the folly of the little town? Why do we yearn for it along with him? This, to me, is the mystery at the heart of Leacock's masterpiece. The book is a paradox. Its purpose seems clear: to skewer the provincialism of small town life, to poke fun at his neighbours – and yet, when we finish that final chapter, what endures is a feeling of affection and a real longing for some simpler, slower, kinder time and place.

I don't believe this effect comes merely from the distance between our time and Leacock's. I suspect the book's first readers felt much the same way when they finished the book soon after it was published in 1912, though I imagine this effect has probably become more pronounced with each passing decade.

I think I understand Leacock's conundrum, though. I grew up in several little Ontario towns myself and itched to grow up and shake their dust from my feet. I couldn't get out fast enough. But time mellows the feelings of the emigrant. The years pass and the sharper edges wear off the memories and become smooth. Even though you recall the sharpness, you strangely end up being charmed by the smoothness itself. Eventually it is possible to be nostalgic for one's own misery. I am fifty years old now and far from the little places of my youth, and still I often find myself taking that long, meandering nighttime train journey into the darkness too.

Seth

*Guelph, 2012.*

**STEPHEN LEACOCK** remains one of the world's best-loved humorous writers six decades years after his death in 1944. Born in England in 1869 and educated in Canada, Leacock went on to be professor of economics at McGill University, from 1908 to 1936. His first collection of comic stories, *Literary Lapses*, appeared in 1910, and from that time until his death he published a volume of humour almost every year. Of these, *Sunshine Sketches* has proved to be his most popular work. Leacock's idyllic summer retreat in Orillia, Ontario, is still preserved as the Leacock Museum, and is visited each year by thousands of admirers.

**SETH** is the cartoonist behind the long-running comic book series *Palookaville*. His books include *It's a Good Life If You Don't Weaken*, *Wimbledon Green*, *George Sprott*, and, most recently, *The Great Northern Brotherhood of Canadian Cartoonists*. He is the book designer for *The Complete Peanuts*, *The Portable Dorothy Parker*, and *The Collected Doug Wright*. The first title in his four-book collaboration with Lemony Snicket, *Who Could That Be At This Hour?*, was published in the fall of 2012.